HAINTS ON BLACK MOUNTAIN

In Ann Hite's beautifully-realized story collection *Haints on Black Mountain*, wandering spirits comfort, enlighten, and sometimes disturb the humans who connect with them. From the forceful figure of Polly Riley determined to preserve her Native American heritage in the opening story, to Gran who does what she must to save herself in the final entry, the characters reveal to us the depth of the human soul. In prose as stunning as the natural world she describes, Hite fills us with the wisdom and wonder of women who inhabit the mountains of Appalachia.

—Susan Beckham Zurenda, award
winning author of *Bells for Eli*

BOOKS BY ANN HITE

NANTAHALA NOVELS

Going to the Water

BLACK MOUNTAIN NOVELS

Sleeping Above Chaos
Where the Souls Go
Lowcountry Spirit
The Storycatcher
Ghost on Black Mountain

NONFICTION

Roll the Stone Away: A Family's Legacy of Racism and Abuse

HAINTS ON BLACK MOUNTAIN

A haunted short story collection

᪅

Ann Hite

MERCER UNIVERSITY PRESS
Macon, Georgia

MUP/ P647

© 2022 by Mercer University Press
Published by Mercer University Press
1501 Mercer University Drive
Macon, Georgia 31207

26 25 24 23 22   5 4 3 2 1

Books published by Mercer University Press are printed on acid-free
paper that meets the requirements of the American National
Standard for Information Sciences—Permanence of Paper for
Printed Library Materials.

Printed and bound in the United States.

This book is set in ADOBE CASLON PRO.

Cover/jacket design by BURT&BURT.

Print   ISBN   978-0-88146-852-6
eBook   ISBN   978-0-88146-853-3

Cataloging-in-Publication Data is available from the Library of
Congress

To Robert Hollis, who left the world before the book was ready for him to read. He was the best reader a writer could have. You are missed. The world has a vacant spot that can't be filled.

◈

In Memory of Robert Hollis
November 27, 2019

◈

Thanks to all the readers who submitted prompts that gave birth to the stories that make up this collection. You inspired the stories in these pages.

Paula Sannar Niziolek
Brigid Firelight
Sandy Coleman Collins
Amanda Grice
Letitia Crawford
Anita Kindrick Bobo
Teresa Martin Gregory
Mary Beth Kosowski
Cindy Pope
Cathy Benedetto
Joy Frerichs
Jalane Rolader
Laura Sharpe Galluzzo
Karen Lynn Nolan
Pat Walker Johnson
Raymond Atkins
Robert Hollis
Sherry Brooks

MERCER
UNIVERSITY PRESS

Endowed by
TOM WATSON BROWN
and
THE WATSON-BROWN FOUNDATION, INC.

Contents

HAINTS ON BLACK MOUNTAIN

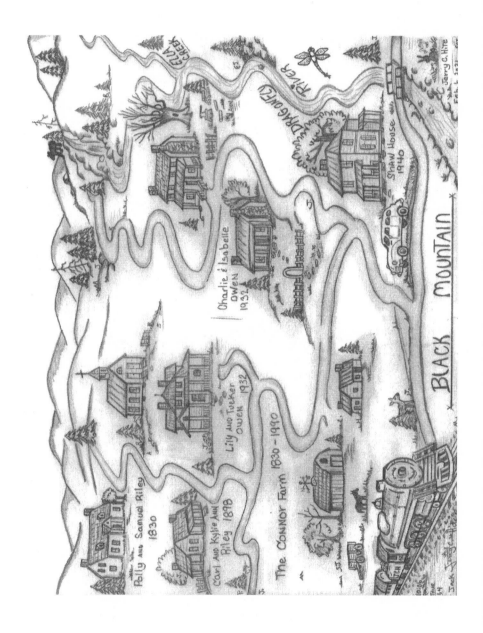

CLEAR CREEK

RIVER

SWITCHBACK

Shaw House
1940

Jerry O. Hite
Feb. b, 1-22

BLACK MOUNTAIN

Charlie & Isabelle
Owen
1952

Lily and Tucker
Owen 1932

Polly and Samuel Riley
1830

Carl and Kylie Ann
Riley 1898

The Connor Farm 1830-1990

Part One

Wind

WRINKLE IN THE AIR

1835

Ireland is blown in with the wind, bringing the salty scent of seaweed, the green of fresh-cut peat. It is swirling down the creek beds and pushing around the trees like a creeping fog, filling these hills with the memory and ache of home. I close my eyes and breathe deeply, letting my soul remember.—Paula Sannar Nizlolek

Souls have always wandered the thick forest of Black Mountain. My elders spoke of their moans that soaked the air in the time between dark and light, a sacred time, a protective time. Who were the souls? I wasn't told this, only that the mountain collected them and would for eternity. But I grew up walking the paths around the mountain, playing in the streams and the river. I could walk them in the black night without decent light. My grandmother called me tree walker. The souls allowed me to be part of their trails. There were times when I was sure footfalls followed me, but when I turned no one was there, just a mountain laurel moving in the stillness. Always I knew they were looking out for me.

I was in my seventeenth year, destined to enter a union with Whiplash Murphy, a Cherokee boy that my parents and his parents decided would serve the tribe best. One day I would be chief, so marriage wasn't about love. This was the year a white man, Mr. Samuel Richard Riley, walked up Black Mountain and brought more of the outside into our world, a quiet, happy place.

❧

The souls moaned louder in the weak light of that one morning. Something stirred behind me and I paused. Black bears could be dangerous if hungry. I turned to look and saw a man with orange hair and beard.

"Excuse me. I didn't mean to scare you." He smiled.

My heart beat in my ears but no words came to me.

"Can you understand me? I suppose you are Cherokee?"

I nodded. My people didn't make a habit of talking to strange men. This man did not belong to the group of families living on our mountain. And his hair was orange, so unusual I thought he might be a soul from the spirit world.

"I'm staying at the Connor farm. Good family. I love these trees." He looked up into the sky, peeking through here and there. He tipped his cap. "Nice to meet you." He walked past me.

The souls cried out, *Be wary of him.*

The man looked around. "Did you hear that?"

A surprised intake of breath escaped from me.

"So you did hear the sound? Was it a strange bird?"

Never had anyone heard the souls but me and one or two elders. "Something like that."

"You speak English."

"Of course." I shrugged.

"Where do you live?" He held a walking stick in one hand.

"On top of the mountain, not far from the waterfall. My family and the tribe have lived on that part of the mountain for as long as elders can remember."

He nodded. "I haven't made it to the top yet."

"The beauty lives at the top." I turned to go.

"I would like to speak with the chief. Could you help me? My friend, Mr. Connor, on down the mountain some,

4

says he doesn't venture to the top of the mountain because of the haints."

"Haints." This was a new word for me.

"Ghosts, spirits."

"Ah yes, they are here with us now."

"Hm. Do you know the chief?"

"We all know the chief of our tribe."

His cheeks turned pink. "Yes, I guess you do. Can you tell me how to meet him?"

"I guess visit like a civilized man."

"When is a good time?"

I shrugged. "I would say to visit at the campfire. Most nights we meet there to talk, to discuss the day, the plans ahead. Much is taking place with the American government wanting our land."

"Thank you, ma'am. What is your name?"

"Polly."

"Nice to meet you, Polly. My name is Mr. Samuel Richard Riley. Maybe we will see each other at the fire."

"Maybe."

And he was gone.

∽

Flames leapt into the night sky. I sat back from the men, but close enough to see Samuel Richard Riley in the glow. His orange hair and beard made him stand out from the group of Cherokee gathered to listen to his tales of a homeland across the great seas.

"These mountains take me back home," he said, gesturing around him. "Every morning before the sun shows itself, the scent of seaweed and fresh-cut peat wakes me. And for a minute, I'm still there on the little farm with the craggy, rocky land stretching in all directions. I forget why I'm here. How important the trip was when I stood before my parents, explaining to them why I was leaving. Why is it I longed for here when I was there, and now I yearn for Ireland so bad my body aches?" Sparks popped into the dark night. Mr. Riley met my stare over Father's shoulder. "And just think, Chief Doublehead, if not for your lovely daughter, I wouldn't have found you and your people. My life's work. This history will be most important, especially now with President Jackson's view on this land. Maybe if people understand your lives, they will see things different." His voice was a soothing balm on a burn, a song in the air, taking me away from the misty mountains and hemlocks that scraped the sky. Listening to him made me forget he was a stranger that knew nothing of our land, and he could never be a savior for our people. The Cherokee would save themselves. This was our land, not America's.

"Polly, Mr. Riley asked you a question." Father turned to look at me.

"I'm sorry. I wasn't listening." I flipped my long dark hair off my shoulder.

"No need to apologize," Mr. Riley said. "I only observed that I had seen you walking the mountain in the early morning—not a question really, an observation."

"I love this mountain like you love your Ireland."

∽

The souls' magic hung in the air, sharp and crisp, cutting into the gray mist that would soon burn away, pulling the voices with it. The dew on the grass clung to my bare feet, turning them numb with chill. Alive. The waterfall roared in my ears. The sky surrounded me on the flat rock that jutted out into the air. I opened my arms in the fuzzy light, where the spirits languished behind the thin haze. A cool breeze swirled and the fresh air washed over me. A whiff of a dream, a way, a new path, stretched through the trees. The sun worked up the side of the mountain as a pink ribbon marking the horizon. The birds, first the catbirds and cardinals, then the sparrows and wrens, and finally the doves and the crows, woke to a new day. The morning sun balanced in the bright blue sky. To the west a hawk shot into the air from a nearby hemlock. Her wingspan stretched wide. Her breast was speckled with rust-colored spots. The sun caught her, glinting off the white. Fresh air stuck in my chest, aching, threatening to crack me open. The sky turned gold and folded the light around me. The heat moved through my bare feet. My grandmother promised that rocks lived just like the flesh-and-blood creatures, and if a girl listened, she would find a message that insisted on being heard.

The hawk dipped close. My heart expanded.

How much do you love this land, tree walker? Enough to sacrifice your wants to keep it? Life on the mountain is changing.

The hawk turned and soared into the sky, straight up to join her friend the sun. The warmth beat on my cheeks and bare arms. The world was still, crystal clear, silent. At my feet was a tulip tree bloom with greenish-yellow petals and a bright orange stripe that circled the base. What was this sacrifice the souls spoke about? Maybe the sacrifice required more courage than I possessed. The bloom grew soft like cloth in my clinched fist.

ॐ

The thick, healthy plants of the healing garden surrounded me, closing off the world. Mother's medicine appeared as a yellow light around her, strong, and every lesson
she passed to me pointed to magic and strength I would one
day own as mine. "Your medicine is balanced on the north
path, the direction of learning and sharing. Your colors are
white and blue, daughter. They shine around you and represent the snow and wind of the north." Mother's touch on my
arm heated. "Close your eyes. See the mountains, how quiet
and calm, feel the light breeze kissing your body. This is the
souls who walk with you. Stay in this calm. This is your
strength, your place in life." Mother's long brown braid hung
down the small of her back, thick like a horse's tail. We were
the same yet different in so many ways.

"You missed these weeds. Where are you today?"
Mother's forehead wrinkled. "Caring for the garden, Polly,
is most important to the whole tribe, to all our people on this
mountain."

"Yes, I know." The restlessness of a thousand girls my
age gathered in my chest. This antsy feeling pushed me to
be something more, better, than the mountain, than the
tribe.

"They depend on us for healing. This is your future.
One day this medicine will be yours alone." Mother opened
her arms to embrace all I could see. "Your life."

My feet, free of the leather shoes that always confined
my step, relaxed in the cool black dirt. My arms stretched on
each side—wings, freedom—encompassed life. A hum of
music filled the air. Mother stopped and listened. "Do you
hear that?"

I dropped my arms and the music stopped. The sound
of a horse broke the spell. The sun's bright light blocked out

a clear view of the rider.

Mother frowned. "Mr. Riley, my husband is in the barn at the back of the cabin." The hoe handle rested against her hand, but the tone of her voice twisted with a strain.

"Good morning, Gu Lu. Your garden is beautiful as always." Mr. Riley tipped his cap.

A straight line on Mother's lips spoke more than any words. "Thank you, Mr. Riley."

He pointed his horse in the direction of the barn but not before turning a smile on me. His gaze burned my face. I studied the mint leaves until the horse walked away.

"This Riley has no respect," Mother fussed.

I dropped to my knees, which grew damp with the dew still lingering on the plants as I pulled the weeds I missed. The fragrances of lemon balm and mint soaked the air. "Why do you say that, Mother?"

"He uses my short name, reserved for those closest to me. He is not a man close to me. He is your father's friend. Not mine. He comes from the north, from across the sea, from a strange land."

"He claims this mountain is like his home." A sprig of lavender relaxed in my fingers.

"I know you are taken with his stories, Polly. This pleasure is written on your face. Half the tribe are captured by his tales. But he has nothing to give us. He will only take. He will be trouble. I see it in the light around him: change."

The peppermint had doubled in size in two weeks. "Is change bad?"

Mother went on without answering. "Your father says his book will help us. His book will tell of our plants, our medicine." Her laugh curled around the edges in a mean way. "He is a fool if he believes this medicine can be learned.

It's not that simple."

"But I'm learning." My voice hung heavier in the air than I intended.

"On some days." Mother knelt over the ginger plants, cupping a small green leaf in her hands. "Polly is amazed with this Riley, but he will not listen to women, especially Cherokee women. He does not value women in the way our men do. She will be happier with a Cherokee man."

"Mother, I'm right here. Please talk to me, not the plant."

"Dear daughter, you do not listen if I talk to you. It is the way of a young woman."

I found the roots of a large clump of weeds and tugged until they were free from the dirt. This was the best tool to rid the garden of pests. The voices of Father and Mr. Riley entered the air before the two men appeared at the edge of the garden.

"Why do they come to bother us?" Mother whispered.

The plants seemed to lean their soft green bodies toward the men.

"Gu Lu, I want you to tell Samuel about our medicine and our ways."

Mother remained quiet.

"You and Polly have the most knowledge. I want you to share with him. I will share the customs and hunting."

"Why should we worry about what a white man thinks? This is our land. We let them settle here, not the other way around. They need to remember this."

Mr. Riley gave a short laugh. A slight rise in his eyebrows showed his disapproval of what Mother said.

Who did this man think he was, laughing at Mother? "It takes more than you can imagine to live a Cherokee life,

Mr. Riley," I said to him. "Stories of your country across the ocean are enticing, tempting, but real life here takes a lot of work and love. Not many have time for writing and pondering others' ways." I shot a glare at him.

Mother turned away to hide a smile.

"I'm sure you have a wealth of information, Miss Doublehead. I will not be a bother to you. I can trail along as you work and walk the forest, of course."

Mother allowed a long breath to escape.

I picked up the water bucket. The wooden handle had splintered and would soon catch the skin of my fingers if I didn't sand it smooth. "I don't know about that," I said as I walked. "You'll have to excuse me. There is water to get from the well for the plants. We are entering our dry time."

"Let me help you." Mr. Riley fell into step with me.

"I'm quite used to drawing and carrying water, Mr. Riley."

"Please call me Samuel. I am so interested in this garden, in your medicine."

"Mother would drop dead in her place if I called you Samuel. We are not so brazen on Black Mountain. My experience with white people is limited to the families here on the mountain, and they don't care to learn anything from us."

"Miss Doublehead, you must forgive me. I've overstepped myself once again. My mother has always accused me of this, and in every letter she points out that this is the reason I still have no wife. She fears I will never manage to have a family. Of course, this would crush her because she has it in her head that I will come back to Ireland to settle down. And there are days I really think I will."

A slight wind picked up. The well stood up the hill behind the cabin. I shook my head. "Is there anything you

11

deem inappropriate to speak about in the presence of a woman?"

"See, I'm an insufferable melter. That means an idiot where I come from." He ran his fingers through his orange hair.

I gave a slight smile and lowered the bucket into the well. The sun glinted on the dark water below. The sky spun, and a picture came to me of a handsome orange-haired boy around my age, wearing pants and a shirt made of cloth I had never seen, odd fitting to him in a tight fashion. Against his ear was a shining rectangle object that he talked into. The bucket slid from my hand, causing the sharp splinter of wood to tear through my palm. The rope unraveled, plunging the bucket deep into the well.

Mr. Riley caught the well handle in a smooth motion. "Are you okay?"

Blood covered my palm. "Yes, a splinter from the handle caught my skin." The image of the boy seared through my thoughts.

Mr. Riley turned the handle and lifted the bucket out of the water. "You look as if you saw a ghost."

"That's silly. Of course I didn't." The vision's leftover clearness clung to me as if the boy had been real.

Mr. Riley wound his handkerchief around my hand. "Would you talk to me about the garden, your life as a Cherokee woman? How it is to have a father who is a chief? Is this medicine they speak of real? Or something that is only lore? Do you want to be here the rest of your life?" His questions peppered me like a weapon. "If you don't want to talk to me, that is fine. I understand. I don't want to make you uncomfortable. But I could learn a lot from you."

"Mother believes you are here to steal our stories and

secrets, that you will only bring us trouble."

He placed the bucket of water on the ground. "Do I look like I mean harm? Maybe when I'm finished with this, I'll go home, find that Irish girl, and make my mother happy."

"You are a storyteller. I am at attention with you. Story-tellers don't always tell the whole truth."

"But you will talk to me?"

"Yes. But Mother will not like it."

The bucket of water sloshed as we walked. "I will take my chances, Miss Doublehead." A laugh laced his words.

⋟

Samuel Richard Riley was close behind, marking my steps, present like my shadow for the next couple of weeks. The souls were strangely silent, as if content to watch us walk through the forest and listen to me tell the stories. When I gardened with Mother, Mr. Riley pulled weeds. Mother even spoke her thoughts.

"What is so special about this medicine you speak of?" Mr. Riley asked. The fuzzy orange hair on his jawline curled more as it grew.

Mother unfolded her body from the spot on the ground. Her shoulders straightened like a ridge of mountains in the distance. "Our medicine is inside each of us. The balance of who we are. This is why some medicine is stronger than others."

An intent look spread across Mr. Riley's face.

"Mother is much stronger in medicine than me because of her wisdom, her experience," I said.

"And my elders are much stronger than me." A rare smile broke out on Mother's face. "Our stories say one must search for the magic lake that holds healing powers. When you are there, it allows you to see things clearly. All things. Polly must receive her true vision, her way, and only then will she know her medicine, her reason to be here."

"Where is the lake?" Mr. Riley asked.

"It could be right in front of you, but if you don't have your eyes open, you'll never see. It's all about seeing." Mother flashed her all-knowing look.

"How are you sure the lake is really there? Where does it come from?" He brushed the dirt from his pants.

"The Great One, the Creator, shaped the world. When he was finished, he stepped back and observed his work. He cried with joy. These tears became the magic lake. The lake we speak of." Mother's whisper landed on the air like sparkling water drops in a splash.

Mr. Riley nodded. "I would very much like to see this lake. I would like to learn how to see it with my eyes."

Mother gave a shrug. "You can't. You don't believe. Only true belief brings you to the lake. Your mind is on other things."

Mr. Riley gave Mother a measuring look. "Very sad, but if I did begin to believe, would I see the lake? I mean, with me being white?"

Mother laughed. "The color of your skin does not close your eyes, Mr. Riley. What closes your eyes is this need to possess others. This is a disease, a war against life. The strength, the knowledge, is inside all people. It is their decision." The tip of her finger pinpointed his chest.

He just looked at her.

"If only we could live our lives on our land. If only we could all exist together. We would all find the lake." Mother looked away as if she saw the lake in front of her.

❧

Later that night, the moon rode high in the sky. *Polly.* The voice broke through my sleep. *Polly.*

I crawled from my bed in the attic and tiptoed outside to see what the souls wanted. The essence of change rode the tingling in the air. Mr. Riley carried the scent of beeswax candles because he read late into the night, and for this reason, I knew he stood behind me before he spoke.

"What brings you out into the night, Miss Doublehead?" He had taken to spending nights in the barn.

"I'm watching the moon. She called to me."

"She? So the moon is a woman?"

"The moon is very much in love with the sun, but for the longest time, the sun didn't know. On the nights that there was no moon showing in the sky, she slipped to the sun in the cover of the dark night. Soon, Sun wanted to know who was this lover coming to him. So the next time the lover came, he took ash from the fire and smeared it on her face. The next night he watched for signs of his lover. Moon hung in the sky, no longer clear and bright but marked with a darkness, the ash." I settled my gaze on the moon. "See, in her embarrassment, she went far away from Sun so she couldn't be caught again. Moon never cleaned the ash from her face in honor of her undying love for Sun, who always waited for her to cross the sky and sink into the trees before he showed himself."

"That's how day and night came about?" Mr. Riley's question twisted in the breeze like glasses knocking against each other.

"Yes, they can never be together because one or the other must give up too much. Poor Moon and Sun."

"Here. I got this from the Connors today. It's meant to be

handed out to all Cherokee." He held a piece of paper. "President Jackson will make the Cherokee walk away from here, far away. He is urging all to do it on their own, but make no mistake: the Cherokee will lose their land."

The paper sat in my fingers, almost hot to touch.

"Father says there has to be a way to keep this from happening, but I can't see what."

"If a Cherokee woman marries a white man, her land becomes his. She and her family will remain there. They will not walk. Since your father is the chief, you technically own all the tribal land in the government's eyes." He stepped back, his eyes glittering in the moonlight. "You could save the land."

A stiff wind blew through and around us. *This is your choice*, the souls called.

"Did you hear that? It sounded like a voice."

"I must think. Stay here."

"But it is dark. You could be hurt." He held out his hand.

"No. Not at all. Wait here." I walked in the direction of the flat rock. The day trapped in the earth still warmed my bare feet. A gust of wind blew straight into me, and the vision of the orange-haired boy flashed through my thoughts. The hawk soaring in the crystal-blue sky linked with my dream at the well. The lake had revealed the future to me. If I chose to marry Samuel Richard Riley, my family would stay on Black Mountain. But my acceptance of his proposal, his deal, would not save our land because he, a white man, would possess it. We, the Cherokee, my mother, my father, me, would still lose. Walk and never be here on my mountain again. Stay and traditions would fall away. I could hope my choice was the lesser evil. Only time would tell.

I turned to find Samuel Richard Riley.

THE ROOT CELLAR

1898

*The wind trained through the building. Crying, we held
on to the sides of the bathtub, me, him, and our two cats.
I can still see the terror in the face of my man, who is
never afraid.* —Brigid Firelight

Love can be blind. That's what the old women in my family
always said. And Lord, I should have listened. But I can only
speak for myself in saying girls never listen to their mamas
and grandmamas when it comes to the subject of men. We
think we know everything.

Carl Riley was the most handsome boy this side of
Asheville, not that I went to Asheville much. He was smooth
speaking and strutted like a rooster in the hen yard.

"Kylie Ann, me and you are going to the ice cream supper together next Saturday night." Carl sat in front of my
house on the back of his daddy's best horse. The Riley family
was up in the world like the Pritchard family when it came
to style, money, and nice houses. Any girl would have been
impressed and honored to be asked to the ice cream supper
by Carl.

"Ok." That's all I could say.

"Be ready at six. I don't like waiting. And wear something pretty. I like yellow."

"See you then, Carl." I gave a wave.

He nodded and rode away.

I stood there for the longest time just watching the dust
settle.

"What you doing out here, Kylie Ann?" Mama stood at the front door. Daddy was out plowing the field to plant our cotton.

"Oh Mama." I grabbed her hands. "Carl Riley just asked me to the ice cream supper Saturday. He'll pick me up at six. I've got to make me a dress that's yellow. He loves yellow."

Mama pulled her hand away and held one up in front of me. "Whoa there. Slow down. I know you're excited, but you hate the color yellow. What are you thinking?"

"Carl likes it. It's his favorite color. I have to have a yellow dress."

"Child, don't go trying to please a man this early. You'll be doing it your whole life."

"Oh Mama, don't be silly. I got me some money. Do you think Daddy will take me to Asheville to at least buy some yellow cloth? I'm not sure I have the money for a new dress."

Mama shook her head. "Come in here. Look at my Sunday dresses. You know I got that pale yellow one I wore back last year for Easter. You just hated the color. I think I can take it up in the waist. You can wear my pearl earbobs."

I threw my arms around her and squeezed tight. "Thank you."

"But remember, Kylie Ann, you got to make a man appreciate you, work hard. Otherwise they'll always think you'll be their doormat."

"Carl's not like that, Mama."

Mama opened the door. "You'd just be surprised. I heard he made Cathy Anderson pay for her ice cream soda when they went to the soda fountain in Asheville."

"You know Cathy, Mama. She's always turning everything serious and worse than it is."

18

When it came time for Carl and me—we was an item by then—to go to the graduation dance, Carl forgot to order my corsage from the florist in Asheville like all the other boyfriends did. He presented me with roses cut from his mama's garden, tied together with some pink ribbon.

"Now those are real special, Carl. You cut them yourself. You did a fine job."

Mama struggled to get the flowers to tie around my wrist.

"Naw, Mama picked them. She said you would like the pink ones the best. I told her you would like her flowers better than store-bought ones."

Mama gave him a stern look.

"Thank you so much. They are special." I gave him a quick kiss on the cheek.

≪⑤

Things between us went along just swimmingly, and by the end of summer after we graduated, Carl started hinting about marriage. "You're a good cook. Wives have to be good cooks. And you're strong. They got to be strong to work in the gardens and out in the fields."

My mama never stepped foot in the field unless it was to get Daddy to come in. Daddy hired someone during planting season. "Well, I ain't a horse, Carl." I know I sounded a little miffed but I couldn't help it.

"No, you're not."

One evening I went to eat dinner with Carl at his parents' house. His mama was the sweetest thing. I helped her wash the dishes afterwards while Carl and his daddy went out to the barn.

"Carl's so stubborn and cheap, Kylie Ann. You may want to find yourself another fellow to marry. He tries the ever-loving patience of Jesus himself. I promise you that. He takes after his daddy's side of the family. Grandma Polly was full Cherokee and didn't waste a thing. She raised her son, Carl's daddy, to think he was royalty. Sometimes I can pinch the both of them for being downright stingy. Grandma Polly couldn't help it. They went through hard times staying here on the mountain when all the others were made to walk. Even her daddy went when he didn't have to so he could be with his people. Polly always favored Carl's daddy because of that red hair. Grandpa had the same hair, and this created a soft spot for her only son. It took me a few years to get Carl's daddy straightened out about how to treat me." Mrs. Riley shook her head. "I just don't want no girl going through what I've been through. Carl has the red hair and he is stubborn. He thinks he knows more than anyone else. I've seen him refuse good direction just to prove he knows better. Think hard before you choose him."

Lord, what kind of mama throws off on her son like that? I let that warning go in one ear and out the other. Carl was going to listen to me. We would be partners, I thought, equal. Sweet Jesus, I had some learning to do.

"Do you, Carl, take Kylie Ann to be your lawfully wedded wife?" The preacher stood with us as a whole church full of folks watched me become Mrs. Carl Riley. I wore my granny's wedding dress.

"I do." Carl looked straight ahead like someone was going to shoot him dead.

"I now pronounce you man and wife." The preacher closed his Bible. "You can kiss the bride."

I threw my arms around Carl's neck and gave him a good kiss. I knew he'd hate me for doing that in front of our guests, but I wanted my wedding kiss. The guests clapped. Carl frowned. "You're embarrassing me."

And so started our marriage.

⁂

"We will have a bedroom in the back with a window looking out at the woods." Carl drew in the dust of the ground, land given to us by his daddy, land where his Grandma Polly once walked. "A kitchen here and a big porch across the front that looks out into the valley." He pointed to a flat rock that seemed to float in the air. "That's where Grandma Polly said yes to my grandpa when he asked her to marry him in the year of 1835. Folks swear they've seen Grandma Polly walking the woods like she did when she was young. I don't believe in haints. Do you?"

Not once had I given haints one bit of a thought, but hearing the story gave me the creeps. "No, but I don't like the thought of folks saying our land is haunted."

"Don't worry. Folks can be afraid of silly stuff. We're fine out here. This land is special."

"I want a root cellar. It would be good for storms." My one big fear was storms. "And it would be good for storing my canning for the winter. You could put me some shelves up around the walls. My granny had one just like that."

"It ain't nothing but a waste of good money, Kylie Ann. We don't have no bad storms up here on this mountain. Kind of hard to have a twister here, don't you think? I can

21

build you a pantry closet to put your canning goods. That will save us some money."

I could have spit nails at that man, but I put a big old smile on my face. "I think one day you'll regret not giving me a root cellar, Carl, just to save you some money."

He shot his lopsided grin at me. "I doubt that, Kylie Ann. I doubt that."

One fact most folks on Black Mountain knew about me was I didn't forget nothing. I was like a dern elephant. One day I would be able to say I told you so.

∽

Just a little past our first wedding anniversary, the granny woman came to visit me. Carl was off working the fields with his daddy.

"Carl and me still haven't gotten in the baby way. I can't figure out why." I had served us tea in fancy little cups. What was I supposed to do when I had to talk about personal stuff?

"Sometimes things happen like this because the man hasn't got any seeds or not enough. It might not even be you, child." Granny Tuggle was her name. She was right smart too. "Your mama had seven kids, Kylie Ann. I doubt you're the one having a problem. And you helped look after your brothers and sisters. Why you wanting a baby so bad? Just enjoy life."

"You have a point, Granny Tuggle."

When Carl came in from working, I met him on the porch. "Granny Tuggle said it must be you that's causing us not to have any babies. I come from a family that had way too many. It can't be me."

Carl frowned. "I want me a son."

I shrugged. "Can't tell you what to do."

The next day I went down the mountain to the Connor farm and got me two tomcats. Lord, I loved them the minute I picked them up. Paul and Earl.

"Look here what I have," I yelled at Carl while he worked at putting a roof on our barn.

"What you got?"

"I got me some cats."

"That's just what we need."

"They ain't going to bother you none. They're mine. Not yours."

"We'll see."

⋘

A few months later I nearly fell over and died. When your husband does something so strange, it can affect you like that. I was baking cookies because it was Valentine's Day. I always did a little something even if Carl didn't thank me or act one bit romantic. He just didn't have it in him. I had finally figured that out. A horrible kind of ruckus took place in the yard. Paul and Earl were hissing and throwing a fit. That had to mean Carl was home early from Asheville. Them cats hated him dearly. I went out on the porch to save him.

There he was with a wagonload of wood and other stuff, but what caught my eye was a white porcelain claw-foot tub. That thing was a beauty. Just as shiny as shiny could be.

"What you got there?"

Carl shaded his eyes with his hand. "Your Valentine's present. Come out here and see."

Now that man hadn't never once in our marriage or

courting bought me one gift. "What you gone and done, Carl? It must be really bad because you've never bought me a Valentine's present."

He shrugged. "What you got to spoil it for? Who said I paid for it? One of them fancy houses down in Asheville was getting a new one. It looks like new. Daddy said he would help me build us on a new room so we didn't have to put the tub in the kitchen anymore."

Not having to take a bath in the washtub in the kitchen sounded lovely. "Ok. I like that idea." Before the week was out, my fancy tub was sitting in a small room built off the back porch. I even had a window. It took a lot of time to haul the water from the pump on the back porch, heat it in the kitchen, and haul the buckets back out on the porch to the little room and pour them in the tub. So I wore myself out before I got that nice, deep, hot bubble bath I'd always dreamed of, but I had a real bathtub almost in the house. This kind of made up for Carl not building me a root cellar. On one of my water trips, I stopped to look at the valley and the flat rock that jutted out into the air. A young woman with long dark hair stood there. Her dress was out of fashion, but honestly that was pretty normal for the mountain. The girl turned and looked at me, threw her hand in the air, and began walking in my direction. Now my bath would be spoiled. She disappeared into the patch of trees separating our hill from the rock.

Carl appeared at the kitchen door. "What are you looking at? I thought you were getting a bath."

"I am. There was a girl on the flat rock. She's walking this way. Watch for her while I put this water in the tub. I've got to start another pot."

Carl was in the yard when I came back on the porch. "I

don't think that girl is coming up here. She must have cut through the woods for home. Who was she?"

"I don't know. Never seen her before."

"That's strange."

⁓

Three days later I was cleaning my tub with the door to the new room open to the fresh air. Sometimes a woman gets a feeling like somebody's watching her, and I whipped around. The young girl I'd seen on the flat rock stood in the doorway. Her eyes were a liquid black, with a look that seemed to stare right through me. Her dark brown hair nearly touched her waist. She wore the same old-fashioned dress. The tomcats, Paul and Earl, both rumbled with purring, which was downright crazy for them.

"There is a storm coming. A bad storm. Watch the sky. Come here to this room. You will be saved. Tell your husband to listen this time." And she was gone. She never turned and walked away. She just vanished before my eyes. I couldn't tell a soul about what I saw. Of course, lots of folks on Black Mountain believed in haints, but Carl and his family sure didn't. I kept my mouth closed.

⁓

Mama Riley—that's what Carl's mama wanted me to call her—had her quilting club every Wednesday afternoon. I showed up on her porch early.

"Well, my goodness, Kylie Ann, you've always been so busy. I'm just tickled to death you decided to quilt with us today. I'll be so proud to have you right beside me."

I fought the urge to roll my eyes. "I'm not much of a quilter. You can ask Mama."

"You just haven't had the right person to learn from." She pulled me into the house. "We got a real special project to start today."

The smell of her chocolate cookies floated through the dining room where the frame was set up. My stomach growled.

"Look right here." She unfolded a quilt of quite some age, a log cabin pattern. "This here was Grandma Polly's first quilt as a married woman." The cloth was soft and faded with lavenders and yellows.

"It's real pretty."

"I want to make a cover to go over it. The thing is almost in threads."

Sadness stuck in my ribs. "Oh, that's too bad. I love it just like it is." I ran my fingers over the threadbare places.

"It's not worth trying to keep warm with now."

"But it's pretty. If it were mine I would fold it at the foot of the bed."

Mama Riley's face turned soft. "I'll tell you what. I'm going to give this one to you. We can just start from scratch."

"Are you sure?"

"Of course I am. Have you ever seen a picture of Grandma Polly?"

I shook my head.

"I can't believe Carl hasn't shown you one. Come here." She led me into her bedroom. "This is Grandma Polly when she was still a young wife."

On the wall hung an oval frame of a beautiful woman. The woman I had seen as a younger girl only days before. The woman who warned me about the storm. My breath stuck in my ribs, and I couldn't speak.

"She was quite the beauty. And so strong. Her husband Samuel loved her better than anything in life. Took her to Ireland after they married to meet his parents."

"This makes the gift even more special, Mama Riley."

"Doesn't it? What makes quilting so special is the stories sewn into them. And it's my understanding that she never liked quilting. This is the one quilt she made." She placed the quilt in my hands.

"Thank you."

"Oh child, this is nothing really, just some old cloth, but I'm real proud you think it is."

⁓

On Good Friday, I sat on my knees in the flowerbed out front of the house, planting some tender strawberry plants that Mama shared with me. The sky had some white clouds racing over the sun, giving me relief from the heat. One would have thought August was on us. The air was hot and sticky. When I stood to stretch my legs, I saw Carl behind the mule, plowing. Across the sky stretched a long black cloud. The air turned greenish-yellow in a matter of seconds. My stomach turned upside down.

"Carl. Look at that cloud," I screamed as I moved toward him.

He unfastened the reins. "Go in the house. Now." He smacked the mule on his haunch. The mule ran to the tree line. Balls of hail began to pelt the ground.

I scooped Paul and Earl into each arm and made a beeline for the kitchen porch. Them cats weren't none too

27

happy about being squeezed in my arms. "Stop your wiggling. I'm trying to save you." They grew calm like they understood me.

"Where you going?" Carl yelled.

"To the tub. It's the heaviest thing we got in the house." He was right behind me.

I crawled in while Carl shut the door. "Get in here with me."

Carl covered me and the cats with his upper body. A freight train barreled right into the house. Part of the tin roof peeled off the new room, with hail making its way inside. Paul pulled out of my crushing grip and jumped from the tub. Carl's arms locked harder around me, keeping me in place. Earl wiggled away and hissed as he jumped from the tub, mewing for Paul.

"Carl," I whispered. A tremor of chills overtook my body.

Trees split and glass broke. The floor shook for what seemed like hours but was surely only minutes. The air grew still and the sound of a single cardinal rang out. That's when I understood that I still had my eyes squeezed shut. A flash of blue sky shone through the tear in the roof.

"We're alive."

Carl placed his forehead on the back of my head and sniffed. He was crying. That grown, tough man was crying like a baby. He kissed the top of my head. "I thought we were goners."

Paul and Earl came ambling into the room through a hole in the side of the wall.

"Those damn cats." Carl laughed.

I stepped over the side of the tub.

"Kylie Ann."

"Yes."

"I'm going to dig us a root cellar. Okay?"

I didn't dare look at that man in the eyes. "Now that's a sound idea."

We walked out of the new room. "Lord, Carl, the house is mostly gone."

"We got to build another one."

"That's all we can do."

⤺

Carl and me grew old in that house together. We had us two kids, a boy named James and a girl named Lily. We used our root cellar many times over the course of our marriage.

One afternoon Carl helped me down the steps as a storm approached. "Carl?"

"Yeah?" He struggled to slide the bolt into locking position. Both James and Lily had been harping on us to move in with one of them, but we wasn't going anytime soon.

"Remember when I asked you to build us a root cellar, and you said it was a waste of money?"

"Lord, Kylie Ann, you ain't never forgotten that. You sure did wait a long time to say I told you so."

"Yes sir. I told you one day you would regret not listening to me." I gave him a hug, and he hugged me back. Carl was a good man, stubborn, but good as good could be.

THERE IS AN UNTOLD STORY

1932

When the merciless winds of March come in like a lion, I am reminded of a night in early March when I was a child. I was awakened by the sound of voices and soft crying down the hall into the living room. My daddy was working the night shift underground in a coal mine, and my worried little body got out of bed, crept down the hall, climbed into my aunt's lap, and said is my daddy dead? To which she just nodded yes, and I understood, more than an eight-year-old should, that he would not be coming home again because the coal mine had taken his life. —Sandy Coleman Collins

Mama thought I was asleep in my bed but not one part of me was tried. The wind caught in the attic and ran through the house like a howling monster that I still sometimes believed lived in my closet. Daddy said there wasn't no such thing. He didn't cotton to any such tales. His feet was planted on the ground, solid and firm. My bed sat under the window in my drafty old room. Outside was a large oak tree with long thick limbs that provided a bridge to the perfect Y of its trunk, where I could sit for hours reading a book on a good day.

The wind kept me in the bed, watching the front yard for dancing haints that came every night to tell their stories. And the only reason I dared watch out the window after nightfall was Daddy, who was late getting home from his job in the Gap, where he worked as a clerk at the train depot. Once upon a time he had been a farmer like his daddy and granddaddy, but the Great Depression walked up the curving road coming out of the Gap and put most of the farmers on Black Mountain in the poor house. A soul would have to believe there was a house for the poor to go to. Most ended up with no home or land. Daddy was blessed to find a job working for the railroad.

As soon as Daddy turned into our long snaky drive, his headlights would flash on my window, glinting, for a second before disappearing behind the trees. The click, click, click of Mama's high heels moved back and forth, back and forth across the polished wood floors of what should have been a fancy dining room downstairs but now had only a shiny cherry table, no chairs.

The wind gathered in the valley and rushed over the mountain—our house was at the top, not far from the old colored settlement that had been abandoned for a good twenty years. Both Mama and Daddy was raised on the mountain. Mama's great-grandmother had been a full-blooded Cherokee. And when it was windy Mama said you could hear the souls moaning for the land stolen from them.

Wind barreled through the trees. I pulled the covers over my shoulder and watched the tall shadows of skinny pines bend this way and that. Two owls called back and forth to each other in the distance. That was a sure sign of tragedy and woe. Then the roaring of the wind grew louder. Pressure pushed against my skull, and just as it seemed my brain would explode, a pounding of rocks began to beat down on the roof. Glass clattered somewhere in the house. A popping sound of gunfire triggered the oak's limb to crack and fall. Gone. The smell of raw wood soaked the air as trees snapped all around.

"Grace, get down here. Run," Mama yelled.

She didn't have to tell me twice. I took the stairs two at a time, burying my face in her dress, the smell of lavender soothing me until I realized her body shook like she had a high fever, and a chill worked through my arms.

"We have to get to the storm cellar," Mama ordered.

To get to the cellar, we had to go outside into the back-yard, open two heavy wooden doors, and go down a flight of stairs into the ground. The house shook. A long, sorrowful moan shuddered through my bones.

Mama gripped my shoulders, digging her boney fingers close to my collarbone. "We're stuck. Where is your daddy?"

The wind stopped as if God heard Mama's question and threw a switch, cutting the power of the storm. Headlights cut through the window in the dining room. I ran to look out. Daddy's truck worked its way over the driveway's steep-est hill, flinging gravel, gears grinding.

"Daddy's here." He unfolded from the cab of his truck.

"Thank you, God, for letting him be okay." Mama smoothed her yellow dress. Daddy glanced at me as he took the first step to the door. His grin was missing.

"You need to go to bed, Grace," Mama said. "The worst of the storm has moved on. Don't you tell your daddy how scared we were. He'll feel bad he wasn't here."

The lights flickered on as she opened the heavy door. "Charlie?" Mama shot me a confused look.

My uncle's eyes had a wild animal look, like when he had way too much to drink and wanted trouble with Daddy. My heart beat fast. "Lily, I got some news. You need to sit down." He waved at the sitting room.

"I thought you saw your father." Mama balled up her fingers into fists.

"Lily, listen to me now. Tucker's dead. Ain't no

33

smoother way to put it." The words filled that front hall like a bunch of them Bible-thumping churchgoers from down the mountain that always thought everyone but them was going to hell. "Dead. That wind just swooped into the Gap out of nowhere and flipped that old truck of Tucker's into the air. The darn thing landed upside down in the river. Must of broke his neck. I got to believe he never had a chance to drown." Uncle Charlie touched Mama's arm, and she jerked it right away like a gunshot hit her. "Don't you worry none. We'll work all this out, Lily girl. I'll help you with all your needs. We're family."

Mama looked at him for a long minute. "Charlie, ain't nothing about you that is family and we both know that. Don't start acting all kind now. Me and Grace will take care of all the arrangements and any problems. We have a home with a roof, and after that storm, ain't no telling how many don't. Take yourself on back off this mountain before your granddaddy's spirit comes after you for being the mean fellow you are." Mama said all this like it had been building in her a long, long time and finally she had released it into the air.

When the funeral director took us in to see Daddy's bluish-gray body, I shivered and shivered until a nice woman took me to sit down. Now, any girl my age would naturally have a hard time with her daddy up and dying in such a horrible fashion. The death part just wouldn't click in my mind. I had seen him with my own two eyes that night.

Mama took me to the junkyard to see the crinkled mess of his truck. I looked away. That truck had come up our drive at the end of the storm. Finally, on the day the beautiful oak casket was lowered into the hole at the old cemetery, something tipped over deep inside me. Daddy wasn't coming back. He wasn't hiding out somewhere. He was dead, gone, left the earth. Mama and me was alone. Forlorned.

I took to the woods every morning, watching for the birds, foxes, hawks, and critters of all kinds. Some days I walked on the mossy banks of Dragonfly River that ran real close to our house. A strong desire to walk off the mountain spread through me. A girl couldn't walk away from home, the place I last seen my daddy. Old folks always said, once a soul left Black Mountain, they never could come back, not really. Just like Uncle Charlie. He tried all the time to woo the mountain, to come back, take his place in the family, but it just wouldn't work. Part of his soul had left him.

While I walked, Mama traveled to a dark, misty, cold, barren place, a place of no return. Her eyes showed a dull void. She got worse and worse. While my sorrow drenched the dust of paths running through the woods, Mama stopped looking after me. Nothing mattered. If I ate or washed was no concern of hers.

"Grace, loving a man will kill you, even if he's a good man. Don't do it. Promise me right now."

"Ok." That's all I dared to say. I had gone from being the kid to being the grownup. "Mama, how are we going to eat? Food is getting low. Letters have come from the railroad. You think they may be about Daddy's money?" I was nine years old, and never had I held any money in my hand.

"We'll make us a garden. Your father can till the ground. I'll plant the seeds."

"What are you talking about, Mama? Daddy's dead. You know that." Mama sat there quiet as if she never heard

35

me. This made chills walk across my scalp. "What about the letters?" I asked.

"Throw them away. He don't need to work there anymore," Mama fussed.

"I'm going to read them first."

"Go on now. I'm tired. I need a nap." She waved me from her bed.

I went downstairs to the kitchen and opened the first letter.

> *Dear Mrs. Owen:*
>
> *I wanted to give you my sincere condolences. Tucker was a fine worker and is greatly missed here at the depot. I was instructed by Mr. Harly Mann, Tucker's boss, to forward this life insurance check to you. I'm sure this will help with moving forward. Included is Tucker's last two paychecks.*
>
> *Sincerely,*
> *Marcus Potter*

I didn't have one clue what to do with the checks. One was for one thousand dollars. Surely we were rich. Maybe I could make Mama talk about what to do with the checks. When I got to her door, she was talking. I put my ear to the door.

"I'm worried about Grace, Tucker. She needs to be with you. I'm afraid she believes this nonsense of your death."

Tears filled my chest. I ran to hide the checks in my room and left the house.

The woods had turned the prettiest green, new green, a beginning shooting out of the dry brush and dead wood of winter. I chose the path deep into the woods. A shadow rounded a curve ahead of me.

"Who is there?" I yelled. But only the birds answered back. "I saw your shadow. I know you are there. Who are you?"

Daddy stepped out of the woods, looking just like he did the night of the storm. "Gracie, you need to get back to the house. Trouble is coming. Your mama needs you. Be brave."

"Don't leave," I said, but he was gone. The cold shrill of fear walked up my spine. I ran back to the house.

No more than five minutes after I came in the back door there was a knock on the front door. Uncle Charlie wore a half smile and gave my dress, that I had worn for too many days, a hard look. I meant to wash some clothes and hang them out, but the days got away from me.

"Where's your mama, Grace?"

"She's in bed feeling poorly."

"Wake her up. We got to talk now."

"No. You'll have to come back another day."

He gave me a stern look.

"Grace, is your daddy down there?" Mama stood on the landing, holding on to the newel post. She was wearing a right pretty skirt, looking more like her old self.

Uncle Charlie pushed his way into the house. "Lily, it's me, Charlie. I've come to take you two with me."

Mama's expression went blank and then pink tinged her cheeks. Three deep wrinkles formed on her forehead. "Why are you here? I told you not to come back. I told you I picked Tucker. I love him, not you. Now go." She pointed to the door.

Uncle Charlie stood two stairs from the bottom. "Lily, you're not well. You're talking out of your head. Grace doesn't deserve to live like this."

37

Part of me loved my uncle for saying this. A weight sat on my shoulders, so heavy I bent over on most days without even noticing.

"You know Tucker wouldn't like this. Folks are asking why I ain't taking care of you. This here is the family farm, been in my family as long as forever, Lily. It's mine and Grace's. I have every right to help you two."

"You ain't getting this house or my daughter. Tucker's coming home anytime, and he will put a stop to you." Mama took one step down.

"Lily, you don't want the court to take Grace away and put her in one of them children's homes. They will put you in the state hospital. You don't want that."

"Leave my home or you will be sorry," Mama screamed with fury.

"Don't you threaten me, woman. I'm not being nice anymore. Come on, Lily. Grace, get you and your mama some things to take with you. Things will get better." His voice sounded kind. Mama had to see reason.

My scalp tingled the warning.

A loud noise exploded. Uncle Charlie wore a surprised look as he crumpled to the floor. Blood, black, spread across his chest like a wicked bloom, spilling onto the steps. A wild look rode in his eyes. His chest shook hard with a breath.

"Mama, what have you gone and done?" I screamed this as my head roared. "He was just trying to help us."

Mama held Daddy's old pistol. "He was going to take me with him. Your daddy would be right mad, Grace. Charlie never has taken no for an answer."

"Daddy wouldn't want you to kill Uncle Charlie. What are we going to do now? They are going to put you away." My words ran up those stairs and slapped Mama.

"Hush up, child." Mama took a few steps down. "We got to get rid of the body. I'll explain it to your daddy." She was calm and smooth like the bit of creek passing behind our house, wandering to the river.

"Folks will come looking for him. He's got friends. People who care."

"They won't know he was ever here. Don't you know a woman without a husband on this mountain is a sitting duck? Men will come out of the woodwork to get what I have."

"This is murder, Mama. All Uncle Charlie wanted to do was help us. And we need help, Mama. Daddy's dead. We got to figure some things out."

Mama gave me a know-it-all smile. "Girl, I know dead. Your daddy ate breakfast with me this morning."

The blood dripped off the stair, puddling on the floor. "Ah Mama, what we going to do?"

"Get rid of that damn body, first. Can we bury it in the woods?" Mama said this like digging a hole deep enough for Uncle Charlie was easy for us.

"I don't see how we can. It ain't right. What about his truck? It's sitting out there for God and everyone to see."

"Ain't nobody going to care about him that much, especially Isabelle. Lord, she probably curses the day she was dumb enough to marry him. He's too partial to shine and other women. You need a truck to drive into town to cash them checks of Tucker's." Her face was clear like a normal person's.

"I can't drive."

"You can learn, Grace. You're a smart girl. We'll tell anyone asking after Charlie's truck, he left it for us. We'll say with Tucker dead, he's gone to find some work." She gave

39

me a half smile. "Let's go dig that hole."

"No, wait. We can't dig it deep enough. Animals will get him and drag him out for all to see. I got a better idea, but what we're doing is a sin. God won't never forgive us."

"Girl, he won't hold it against you because you're just minding me. That's what you're supposed to do. You let me deal with God. What's your idea?"

"Let's take him to the old well. We'll push him in." This meant I had to touch my dead uncle. How could I? His body was still warmish, and I tried not to think. "Get his ankles."

Mama's face lit. "Good thinking, Grace."

My knees nearly buckled.

"Come on. Do you want your mama to go to prison?"

I pulled him as Mama lifted his legs. A long smear of blood followed us out the door, across the porch, and into the yard.

⁓

Daddy always said don't go walking too early in the morning 'cause you might fall right off the mountain, seeing how the light is fuzzy and the mist could be thick. The truck engine started on the first try. I moved the stick like I'd seen Daddy do a million times on his. We couldn't keep the damn truck. People wouldn't believe Uncle Charlie gave it to us. I pressed on the gas and jerked forward. I inched the truck onto the old road, really just a path. Nobody ever drove up to the top of the waterfall. I stopped right at the edge. For a second I thought how much easier things would be for me if I just went on over the side with the truck. But I put the thing in gear and jumped out. The truck jumped forward and then rolled over the side. The last thing I saw of that truck, it barreled into thick brush way down the side, hidden. When I turned to go, Daddy stood right there.

"Gracie, you can't hide what your mama did forever. One day someone will come looking for Charlie, and there won't be no stopping the story. A soul can't hold something so dark a secret forever." He looked so real. Maybe he was alive. Or maybe I had lost my mind.

"Now, Gracie, you need some money. I put some in a jar out in the barn, in my granny's trunk. Get it. Go down to Mr. Connor's farm and get him to help you with the checks. He's a good man, quiet. He won't tell your business or ask you questions. Understand?"

"Yes sir."

"You're strong. Hold on to this. I'll always be here. In the wind, blowing in the trees. Watching after you. Looking after your mama." And he was gone.

I never saw him again, but Mama did. It was the magic of talking to him that saved her, kept her calm. Magic with a horrible dark secret.

Some might not believe in magic, but I do. I hear it moaning in the wind each night as I go to bed. I see the shimmering edges as I look out the window. Watching. Watching for the next storm to blow in. 'Cause there has to be one coming. Sometimes I catch a sideways scent in the air. That big storm is coming one day, and that's when I'll know it's time to tell my story. The wind will blow across this mountain and the untold story will be finished. I'll finally be at peace.

SHE'LL COME HOME WITH THE WIND

1932

For me the March wind was the finishing touch before a reconnection with my daughter last year. It had been a heartbreaking journey of three and a half years that was finally about to blossom into a prayer answered, beyond what I could ever imagine. —Amanda Grice

I knew better than to marry Charlie Owen, but love just got the best of me. That and I was almost thirty, a spinster in most people's eyes, destine to grow old taking care of Daddy. Charlie and I met at Daddy's store down in Asheville. He was buying some hinges for his mama's screen door.

"You need the heavy-duty ones for a screen door. It gets used so much." Daddy held out the shiny silver hinges to Charlie, who took them.

"Do you have any canning jars?"

"Yes we do. Just got some new ones in. What size?"

"Quarts."

Daddy looked at me behind the counter. "Isabelle, can you get us a box of quart canning jars in the back?'

"Sure. Give me just a minute." I smiled real nice at Charlie. He was a customer.

He gave me a nod.

When I came out of the back room, Daddy was talking to Widow Parsons. "Here you go." I handed the box to Charlie.

"Maybe I'll get on Mama's good side now." He winked. "I still live on my folks' farm. She don't much care for me coming home smelling of shine."

My cheeks heated up. "I guess not."

"Do you still live at home too, Miss Isabelle?"

"If you're asking whether I'm attached, I'm not." I smiled again as I counted his money at the counter.

"Well, I'm Charlie Owen. You should come to my church's social Sunday afternoon. Lord, Mama will fall over dead with me crossing the threshold of Black Mountain Church for the first time in only Jesus knows how long." And that was that.

Charlie and mostly Daddy built us a little house on the land Daddy bought from my new father-in-law. The house was right cute, yellow with a little fenced-in yard. Before I knew it, Bell, our baby girl, was born. By then I knew I was stuck as stuck could be with a man who was dead set on drinking himself to death. I poured my life into that beautiful baby girl. Charlie stayed away more than at home. Suited me just fine. I worked for Daddy at the hardware store. By some miracle he had kept it open for business after the Depression hit, but he barely broke even. Mrs. Owen, Charlie's mama, watched Bell for me. This wasn't perfect since she didn't much care for me, but she loved Bell almost as much as she loved Charlie.

That morning in late February gave off heat like a July day. Mrs. Owen stood on her front porch as I pulled Daddy's truck into the yard with baby Bell.

"You're outside early this morning." I chirped my fake sing-song greeting.

She frowned. "Nothing good about a hot winter morning." Her face broke into a smile when she reached for Bell. "How's Nana's little girl?"

Bell cooed and laughed.

"I may be just a little late. We are doing inventory at the store."

"A mama's place is in the home, not working in a hardware store. I'd think your daddy would think that too."

Resentment and anger bubbled under my fake smile. "Well, Bell and I have to eat."

"Times are hard. That daddy of yours is making money. He could give you what you needed. We're struggling here. If it wasn't for the garden and Tucker getting that job with the railroad and helping his parents, we'd starve. Poor Charlie is beside himself worrying about you two. He said you chased him off last week."

"He came in drunker than a skunk, throwing the chairs around. I had to get Tucker down to do something. I can't have him in my house drinking, especially around Bell."

Mrs. Owen patted Bell's back. "Did you ever think you're running over Charlie? Like you just said that house was your house."

"Mrs. Owen, I've done everything I can for Charlie. He's the one running over me. I'll be home as soon as I can." I kissed Bell on the top of her head. "Bye, baby girl. I love you." She laughed.

As I climbed into the cab of the truck, a voice floated over my shoulder. *Don't leave her today. Go get her.*

Mrs. Owen opened the screen door to walk in.

"Watch Bell real close today," I yelled.

The woman glared at me. "What do you mean? I watch her close every day."

"No, I don't mean that. I have an odd feeling. Don't let Bell out of your sight."

"I never do and I'm bothered you think I do. You're talking crazy just like Charlie says you do." And she went in the house, carrying my beautiful baby with her.

I drove down the mountain to the store thinking about the voice. I must have imagined the whole thing. Somehow I had to figure out a way to take care of Bell and work at the store. Get her away from Mrs. Owen. This was a mean thought. She had been nothing but a good grandmother.

∽

The hot wind was whipping around when I left the store an hour later than normal.

"You be careful, Isabelle. Feels like a bad storm coming."

"I will, Daddy."

On the way out of town, I stopped at the train station. Tucker Owen was in the little office behind the ticket window. He smiled and stood when he saw me. "Hello, Isabelle. Is everything okay at home?"

The poor man was so used to me calling him about Charlie, he thought there was trouble every time he saw me.

"All is fine. I'm just heading to pick up Bell from your mama. She's been talking to Charlie, so he's around."

"That doesn't surprise me none. He's always went running to her when he's in any kind of trouble. I heard he has a gambling debt to someone here in Asheville that won't let it go. Be careful."

"You think they'll come to the house?"

"Probably not. I'm sure this man knows Charlie isn't

spending time being a husband and father. But just be careful."

Unrest crept through my bones. "I will. I'd better go. You better head home. There's a storm coming."

Tucker glanced at the clock. "I leave in an hour. Remember what I said."

When I pulled into Mrs. Owen's yard, it was dark but I could see the trees whipping. The truck door was hard to open. Again Mrs. Owen met me on the front porch.

"She ain't here. She's with her daddy and you won't be knowing where that is, so put her out of your mind."

I ran across the yard. "What? What are you talking about? Where is Bell? I want her now."

"I said she's with Charlie. He'll bring her home by tomorrow. That's what he said."

"You just gave him my girl?" The anger filled my chest.

"She be his girl too, Isabelle. He has a right."

"Don't you care about Bell? Don't you care what could happen?"

"Her daddy loves her. You can't keep his own child from him. Go on home. He'll bring her back in the morning. Go on now." She looked at my balled fists.

"Do you even know where he went in this weather? You're horrible. I'm going to the sheriff."

"Girl, what you going to tell him? That Bell's daddy took her off somewhere? You think the law will stop him? You're just a wife with no real say-so. Your daddy just raised you all high and mighty. Go on home. He'll bring her back tomorrow."

"And if he doesn't, Mrs. Owen, if something happens to my baby, the deed is at your feet."

"Go. Now." She stomped in the house.

What could I do? I turned the truck toward the house. Maybe Charlie was there. Where else would he take Bell? He had to be at home. But when I got there, the yard was empty and the windows were dark. I jumped from the truck.

The sound of a train coming toward me filled the space. My dress blew as if it might tear off my body. "Where's my baby? I need my girl! God, please help me."

The little fence pulled out of the ground and was carried away. "He could be anywhere." The wind swallowed my scream. A woman, or a girl, with long dark hair stood on the porch. I ran to her. "Do you know where my baby is?"

The girl never opened her mouth when she spoke. "She'll come home with the wind." And she was gone. The oak in the front yard split in two and rumbled the ground when it fell. The old barn splintered into pieces.

I opened the front door and it fell off the hinges. Trees began to fall everywhere. It was the end of the world. All I wanted was my Bell.

∽

The morning dawned with mist hugging the mountain. I was on the floor of the sitting room looking out the window. Daddy's truck was crushed by the big oak. The granny woman, Maude Tuggle, rode her horse into the yard.

"Anyone here?"

Maybe she knew. "I am." I ran out on the porch.

"Are you okay, Isabelle?"

"Yes, but Charlie, my husband, took our baby girl. I need to find her."

"The mountain is a mess. You can't get down or up. I've heard bad news. Mrs. Connor says Tucker was killed in the

48

storm in Asheville last night. The wind flipped his truck into the river." She gave me a long look. "Mrs. Connor said her husband heard it from Charlie."

"Tucker's dead? That just can't be. But Charlie is on the mountain. Did he have Bell?"

"I'm sorry, Isabelle. I don't know. If you go looking, you'll have to do it on horseback or foot. Be careful."

"I'll go to his mama's. Or maybe Tucker's." Hope bloomed in my chest. "Thank you, Miss Tuggle."

"Just be careful. I'm sure Charlie isn't far off with Bell."

"I will."

⌀

I took my old mare and saddled her, making my way down the mountain a piece. My in-laws' house was missing. For a minute I was sure I'd gotten lost trying to get there. The land seemed altered. No wood, no roof pieces, not even a broken window. Just a few field stones that had held the house off the ground. But I saw their barn in the distance.

"Mr. Owen...Mrs. Owen? Charlie!" Only songbirds answered back. "Hello, are you here?" Charlie's truck wasn't there. When I got close to the barn, the door squeaked open. Mr. Owen came out. "There you are," I said. "Is everyone okay? Have you seen Charlie?"

His eyes were dull, as if he wasn't listening, as if he was a walking dead person.

"Mr. Owen, can I help you? Is Mrs. Owen okay?"

He finally saw me. "I can't find her. We were both in the kitchen when the storm hit. I can't find her."

"Oh no. Have you seen Charlie?" I did my best to hold in the fear because if I allowed it space, there was no telling what would happen.

"I seen him long enough to hear Tucker died. He was on his way there to tell Lily and Grace. He hasn't been back. I told him his mama was missing. I tried walking in the woods but it was so dark and so many trees are down. The house is gone…I think the storm took it and the Missus."

"Don't say that. She has to be here."

"Young lady, if she was here, I would have seen her."

"Can I do anything for you? I'm looking for Charlie. He has Bell."

"Naw, he didn't have her last night." He shook his head and turned to go. "You shouldn't've ever married that one. He's nothing but trouble. The only one who believed in him was his mama." He walked back in the barn and shut the door.

"Mr. Owen, please tell Charlie I'm looking for him."

⌁

What about Daddy? Did the storm get him? The trees had been cut and cleared from the road. I made my way down the mountain. The Connor farm was the first house I could see from the road. Mrs. Connor held the ladder for her husband as he worked on replacing boards that had been ripped off the side of the house. The kids running around the yard dug into my heart. I waved.

"Isabelle," Mrs. Connor called.

I rubbed the mare's mane, jumped off, and came to where Mrs. Connor stood. "I'm so glad to see your house standing." My voice broke.

"I hated hearing about Tucker. That is just terrible."

"Yes ma'am, it is. Grace is not but nine. Can I ask you a

question?"

"What is it?"

"How did you find out about Tucker?"

Mrs. Connor gave me an odd look. "Why, Charlie told Bill."

"When did you see Charlie?"

Mr. Connor looked down at me. "I helped clear the trees so he could get up the mountain. He told me he had to get to Lily and tell her about Tucker. And check on you and Bell."

My heart raced. "I haven't seen him. He took Bell from his mama's yesterday when I was at work. Mrs. Owen is missing and my father-in-law isn't talking straight. He's beside himself. I'm going to Asheville to get Daddy and see if he can help find Bell. The oak in our front yard fell on the truck."

Mr. Connor crawled down the ladder. "I'll take you."

"Oh, I can't ask you to do that. You have things to take care of."

"You didn't ask, child. We have to help you find that baby." Mrs. Connor touched my arm, and I thought I would break down crying.

⁓

The mountain was in a mess, but Mr. Connor was able to work his way down the road. A car came at us from the other direction as we turned off the mountain.

"Stop. That's my daddy." I waved out the window.

He pulled up beside Mr. Connor's truck. "Isabelle, is that you in there? Lord, I been so worried."

That's when the tears came in floods.

Daddy got out and came around to help me out of the truck.

"I was taking her to find you," Mr. Connor said in his calm, sure voice. "We was hit pretty bad up here. Charlie hasn't been home. His brother is dead, his mama's missing, and Isabelle can't find Bell. She's worried sick. She was going to ride her horse to find you."

"Thank you, Mr. Connor, for looking after my girl. We'll piece this together."

Mr. Connor gave me a wink. "That baby will be home before you know it. Nothing is wrong with her."

But how could he even know?

"Of course she will," Daddy said. "Come on, Isabelle." He opened the door on his car. "Can I make it back to her house in the car?" he asked Mr. Connor.

"I think the road is clear now. Most of the way."

"Thank you again."

Daddy had to pull the car over close to the house and move part of a tree out of the road. "Now, what happened?"

I poured out everything. How I got back to Mrs. Owen and what she said. "Our barn is gone, too."

"We can build another barn, but I got to find that no-good husband of yours. When we do, that baby girl will be there."

"I hope so."

Daddy put the car in gear. "You got to believe, Isabelle. Now go on in."

When I got out Daddy stayed in the car. "You go on in," he said again. "Get some wood for a fire. Make you some supper. I'll be back. I'm going looking for Charlie."

"I'll come with you."

"No, you need to be here in case he comes to drop Bell

off." But we both knew that wouldn't happen.

⁓

I spent the next week waiting, watching, praying, and crying. Daddy searched everywhere. "Nobody has seen him," he said, shaking his head. "What about his brother's wife? Should I go over there?"

"I don't think he'd be there. Lily doesn't like him."

"I'm going to check anyway."

"I'm going too. I need to see Lily and Grace. I'm sure I missed the funeral."

"If you don't think Charlie will come by here."

Tears blurred my vision. "Daddy, he ain't never bringing her back here. He wants to punish me. Mrs. Owen told me that. Or pretty much."

"When I find him, there will be hell to pay."

Tucker's house looked the same as always, except there were trees down everywhere. I knocked and knocked on the door, but no one came. But then, as I was walking down the front steps, Grace came out of the woods.

"Grace, where is your mama?"

The child gave me a small smile. "She's probably still asleep."

Under my foot, a dark brown trail was going down the stairs. "I wanted to check on you two. I'm sorry I missed the funeral. I'm waiting on Charlie to bring Bell home. He took her before the storm and hasn't come back home."

Grace's face turned pale. "I ain't seen him, Isabelle. He was here the night of the storm. Mama told him to leave and not come back."

"Well, if you see him, tell him I need to know where

Bell is." My voice broke.

"I ain't seeing him, Isabelle. He won't come bothering us." She said this in such a way I couldn't help but believe her. "Your baby girl will come home. Charlie wouldn't hurt her." Grace said this with such conviction I wanted to believe her. "He's a mean drunk, but he wouldn't hurt children. That's what Daddy always said about him."

And I knew she was right about that. Charlie wouldn't hurt Bell. But he might never bring her home.

Another week went by and I was sitting on the front porch in a kitchen chair, watching. Just watching. That's what I did when Daddy was gone looking. He had been to the sheriff, but nobody had heard of a lost child being found. Charlie was gone. And I didn't let my mind go to the place where it kept drifting.

I just watched. The sky had a way of looking different in a matter of minutes. The cardinals had begun to build a nest. The flash of red is what drew my attention. And then I saw dust billowing on the road below. I figured Daddy was back. I stood. The wind came out of nowhere, a gust that felt like it might pick me up. A dark red car came up the drive. I walked down the porch steps.

A flashy woman wearing a blue hat with little pearls sewn into the net got out of the car. Her lipstick was a perfect red. Her dress matched her hat. "Ma'am, I hate to bother you, but the man on the next farm over said you knew Charlie Owen."

My ears roared. "Yes. I'm his wife."

She laughed. "Well, that just figures."

"Have you seen him?"

"No, though I wish I had. I'd give him a thing or two. But seeing you explains everything. I have something for you in the back seat."

I walked out to the car as the woman opened the door. "Oh, my good Lord."

Bell opened her eyes and reached out to me.

The smell of her head next to mine was the best thing ever. "Thank you, thank you. How did you get my baby?"

"Charlie left her with me the day of the storm. He promised he'd come back to get her the next morning. He said he was babysitting her for his sister-in-law because she was sick. I thought who in the world would let Charlie Owen babysit, but like some fool, I believed him. And she is such a cutie." She touched Bell's head. "Charlie Owen with a kid. You can just blow me over." She paused and looked around, pressing her hat down on her head. "This wind is terrible up here."

❦

Later that week, some boys had gone fishing and found Mrs. Owen's body way out near the river where the storm left her. I moved back in with Daddy and left the house empty, just in case Charlie ever came home. But I knew he wouldn't. He never did.

THE BEGINNING, THE MIDDLE, AND THE END

ATLANTA 1986

March, I prayed to get to March. The worry of not carrying twin boys to term made me anxious, and day-to-day life at home with three others was anxious enough, without worrisome thoughts of bringing preemies into our crazy, dysfunctional world. You see, in the beginning, they began as three, unbeknownst to me, so losing the one made the two remaining babes even more precious.—Letitia Crawford

The wind or a tornado blew away my grandmother's home when she was a child, injuring her sister severely. Fast-forward fifty years, and every time the upstairs windows rattled when a storm may or may not be blowing in, we had to go to the storm pit or cellar. The problem was we could never find our own clothes in her rush to the cellar. I would wind up in my aunt's shirt, my uncle's britches, and shoes so big they fell off before we stepped off the porch.—Anita Kindrick Bobo

In the beginning there were three, 1, 2, 3 beautiful boys, snuggled inside my uterus. I was born Gifted Lark, named by hippy parents who now lived three states away from me. On the January morning when I saw my first ghost, my husband Doug had been working in South Georgia near the Florida state line for nearly a week. In our little double bed, his absence left a vacant place that filled most of my thoughts. There was something to be said for the warmth a spouse's body gives to a cold, leaky rental house. But a paycheck kept the roof over our head.

Moisture had frozen on the inside of the big living room window, with ice so thick I couldn't see outside. *Trapped* was the word that kept jumping in and out of my thoughts. Trapped in the three-bedroom home with two children and three on the way. Unknown to me was the fact that they were all boys. The technology to tell the gender was there but rarely used.

"Sit on the sofa and watch TV. Get inside your sleeping bags."

Hunter, my six-year-old son, and Connie, my five-year-old daughter, obeyed, which was a miracle. Schools were closed due to the subfreezing temperatures. The furnaces all over the city were overworked, tired, and threatening to quit. Atlanta was virtually shut down. Grandma Anna, in Black Mountain, North Carolina, would have cackled at the thought of a whole city closing due to cold temperatures. She was fearless. Nothing but thunderstorms stopped her from carrying on her daily life. She pretty much raised me until I was twelve and my parents turned conservative and settled down. According to the news that morning, Western North Carolina was experiencing colder weather than we were.

I switched on the television. "Since you're not going to school, you can watch the space shuttle take off."

"Oh, Mom. I don't want to watch that. It's too boring. Let me play Mario," Hunter whined.

"Me too." Connie had my crystal-blue eyes.

"Maybe after the shuttle takes off," I promised, adjusting the rabbit ears to get the picture to straighten. With two kids, three on the way, and one income, cable was impossible, a pipe dream, pie in the sky. Guilt washed over me.

"You'll enjoy this. It's important history being made."

"Yeah, I know. My teacher said the same thing."

A slight cramp moved across my back. I left the kids and went to the bedroom. The bed nearly filled the floor space. The icy wind shook the tree limbs, rattling them like bones. The sky was so blue, my tears threatened to fall. Most days I wanted to cry. What if the babies came too early? What was too early for triplets? And what was the heaviness that had settled in my womb, and what about my tilted uterus, so tilted that the doctor described it as upside down? If only Grandma Anna was nearby. She claimed to have a knowing that allowed her to see when something bad was headed her way. Her second great-grandfather Samuel Richard Riley built a big, rambling house on the site of his wife's family home. Grandma Anna had come to live there in the forties and never left. Plenty of room for a granddaughter and great-grandchildren. But Doug would miss us too much.

Another cramp moved around my back. I folded into the thick comforter. Maybe if I slept for awhile the weighted feeling would disappear.

Black Mountain, 1942

Anna Marie looked at her grandmother's house. The grand-mother she had never met. The house was huge and sat high on Black Mountain in the state of North Carolina. Anna Marie, twelve, and her sister Louann, ten, sat in the backseat of the family car.

"Your father played in this very yard," twittered Mama. Her beautiful black heels sunk into the soft, soggy grass. "The dirt here in the spring will swallow you whole. That is what I remember the most about my few visits." Mama leaned through the open car door. "Get out, girls." She worked her heels out of the mud.

"The spring thaw always makes the land into its own being," croaked a bony, wrinkled woman standing on the edge of the large front porch. "You can just call me by my given name, Sally. Seeing how we never laid eyes on one another. We'll work up to closer names later."

Anna Marie studied this grandmother, who lived alone and had done so for years according to Mama.

Sally peered back at Anna Marie. "You look so much like him. He couldn't have had a boy that looked as much like him." There was a softness in her tone.

Daddy was somewhere in Germany fighting for freedom, and no one had heard from him in months. Mama kept saying that was normal, that letters had a hard time tracking down soldiers. Sometimes Daddy's face disappeared from Anna Marie's thoughts. And the sound of his voice evaporated more each day.

Sally looked Mama up and down. "These girls are soft. They may have a hard time living here on the mountain."

Mama's expression dropped. "It won't be for long, Sally. I know it will be hard with them around. I promise I'll find a job and get our own place." She glanced at Anna Marie and Louann.

A big smile revealed Sally's perfect set of teeth. "Lord, I ain't trying to get rid of them. The more the merrier. They just going to have some trouble settling in." She looked down at the girls and spoke to them. "Your daddy was a handful with all his friends coming and going. Lord, once I found the whole lot of them on the barn roof. It was a wonder they didn't die falling off. We ain't a bit fancy here. And there are some girls and boys on the mountain. Maybe you can make some friends."

Anna Marie fell in love with Sally in that moment when she handed her small slice of hope. "Me and Louann will be fine. I promise."

"Well, get your stuff then. We got so much room in this house it's scary. You'll have to dust and clean the rooms you want. The whole upstairs belongs to the two of you."

Anna Marie squeezed her sister's hand. Louann smiled, showing that space between her two front teeth that she got from Daddy.

"Well, girls, let's get those bags." Mama followed Anna Marie and Louann to the car. When the bags were deposited on the front porch, Mama opened her arms wide. "Kisses for me."

Anna Marie clung to her. "Don't go," she whispered in Mama's ear.

"I have to go. There's no place to work here. I'll be back as soon as possible. Write me when I send you my address. No worrying." She let go of Anna Marie. "Thanks, Sally. Here is my parents' phone number for an emergency."

Sally took the paper. "The closest phone is Maude Tuggle. She's the granny woman down the mountain a ways. Won't be calling unless the sky falls."

Atlanta, 1986

"Mom, the shuttle will blast off in just a minute." Hunter stood at the door of the bedroom.

Had I fallen asleep? One of the babies kicked hard. "Oh goodness. I can't miss that." My hands ached with cold. Was the heat working? The hum from the hall suggested it was running. For a minute, I looked out the window still fogged with ice, the light bright like a summer day. Doug would call soon. He always called before lunch when he was out of town.

"Did you know there's a schoolteacher on this space trip?" Hunter asked.

"I saw that on the news. She's been training with the astronauts. Her whole class is supposed to be there to watch this morning." I went to sit with Hunter and Connie on the sofa. "The shuttle is taking off from Kennedy Space Center in Florida. I wonder how cold it is there."

"Cold, Mama. They said much colder than ever before." Connie snuggled up to me. A pain ran across my back.

"I'm sure they're feeling very cold, then." Maybe a call to the doctor would be a good thing. Just to make sure the pains were nothing.

"Do you think the teacher's class is worried about her?" Connie asked. "Space is far away from school. Is she a mom? Is she married?"

I smoothed her hair and gave a shiver. "I'm sure everyone is frightened for her, but isn't she brave? This is the first time someone who isn't an astronaut has gone into space. How could she not go? Her parents will be there too, watching."

"She has a mom and dad. Wow."

I had to laugh. "We all have moms and dads, Connie." I squeezed her shoulder. "And just because you are grown doesn't mean your parents aren't your parents. They will always be your mom and dad."

"That's good. Will you always make sure I wear my gloves and hat when it's cold?"

"I'll always worry about it. That's what moms do." What would Hunter and Connie be like when they were grown?

What would these sweet babies be like? I touched my stomach. Three.

"They said the shuttle might not take off because of the temperatures. That's why they're late." Hunter spoke like such an old soul.

Was the world too crazy to be raising children? Had Mama felt the same way when she was carrying me? Did she feel that at any moment all the things that gave me pleasure could implode and leave me alone to deal with leftovers?

"The countdown." Hunter jumped to his feet.

The babies stirred as if they could hear their brother. Part of this family already.

"Liftoff. Liftoff of the twenty-fifth space shuttle mission, and it has cleared the tower," the news anchor said in his reassuring voice.

"Listen to them cheer. Look, there's the class." Hunter jumped up and down. "I wish I was in that class."

"Wouldn't that be fun." I laughed. Maybe the pains in my back were nothing to worry over. After all, I was the size of a woman about to have a full-term baby, but it was two months early. The space shuttle moved higher into the cold, blue winter sky. "I need to call the doctor, kids. Though they might not even be in the office today." I could call Doug if there was a problem, but there was no problem. Everything was going just like the doctor said it should.

The fire shot from the boosters and the shuttle rolled to its side.

"Wow, Mom, is the shuttle supposed to do that? Did it explode?" Hunter yelled.

A fireball with a lot of white smoke traced its way across the sky. The *Challenger* was not visible.

"Where's the shuttle, Mom?" Hunter cried.

"Mommy, are they okay?" Connie asked.

I couldn't move. My mouth went dry.

The news anchor seemed puzzled. "Maybe one of the boosters had problems. They plan for stuff like this."

I couldn't tell what was happening. A controller at Kennedy Space Center kept saying this was a big malfunction, his voice very calm, as if he were trained not to reveal too much emotion. No one understood what was taking place.

"Mom, I think the shuttle is gone," Hunter said.

A hard gust of wind hit the living room window facing the street and rattled the glass. My balance disappeared and the room spun in the most peculiar way. A click sounded in my body and water began to gush.

"No. No. I need to go to the hospital."

Hunter and Connie's faces turned pale.

"I think the babies are coming." A more intense pain shot across my back. "Let's get in the car."

The camera captured an older couple. The woman wore an expression of pure sorrow. The teacher's mother. She knows, I thought. Mothers always know about their children. "We have to go," I urged.

The old car battery made a slow, dragging sound. "Not now," I groaned. "Are you kids covered up?" Another pain shot across my back and circled my stomach. "Please God, make this car start." Triplets needed to be born in the hospital, especially when they were early. The battery groaned again, finally firing to life. "Thank you." The car engine chugged and smoothed as it warmed. The heat moved into the car. "Maybe this will warm the car soon." Again a pain, the worst yet, shot from back to front. Only one minute had passed.

I eased the car out of the driveway and onto the road.

Another pain. The fuzzy feeling of letting go of control moved through my body. I saw Grandma Anna standing outside the Burger King. She wore her faded housedress and waved at me. I pulled into the parking lot. Another pain pulled hard.

"I need help, Grandma Anna. I need help now."

Hunter, my brave little boy, jumped from the car and ran right through Grandma Anna into the restaurant dining area.

Black Mountain, 1942

"Children have to keep busy and not with foolishness. Washing dishes, learning to sew, and baking a cake are only a few things on your list to learn, girls." Sally gave a chuckle. And she kept the sisters working on a job all day.

A week or so after the girls had come to live on Black Mountain, a long, dark cloud came rolling over the horizon. Winds shook the trees. Anna Marie stood at the tall window in the bedroom she and Louann had chosen together.

"Girls, get down here now. Right this minute," Sally yelled in a new voice. Was she scared?

"Something must be wrong," Anna Marie said to Louann. "Let's go." She looked at her sister's stocking feet. "Put on your shoes."

Anna Marie ran to the door as Sally screamed again. "Now, girls! We have to go to the storm cellar."

Louann ran in front of Anna Marie and down the stairs, clumping in Anna Marie's Sunday shoes.

"Why have you got my shoes?"

"I couldn't find mine."

Sally met them at the bottom. "Let's go. It's a twister."

White balls of ice beat the ground as they all ran down the porch stairs, Sally leading them to the double wooden doors that led to the cellar, a place Anna Marie had no desire to see. But she entered in a flash after the door opened, pulling at Louann's dress hem to keep up. The dark was thicj, and Anna Marie couldn't see her hand in front of her face. A warm yellow light filled the clean and neat room. Shelves of canned goods lined the walls. Four straight-back chairs sat in the middle of the room.

"We're safe now." Sally looked the girls up and down. Her gaze stopped on Louann's feet. "Where is your shoe, child?"

Anna Marie looked at her sister. "What happened to my other shoe?"

Louann hung her head. "It fell off when I jumped off the porch to get to the cellar quicker."

"Those were my good shoes," Anna Marie fussed.

Sally laughed. "Lord, you two are just a mess. Sit down here and I'll tell you a story about a girl who was afraid of storms." She looked at Anna Marie. "We'll get that old shoe when the storm's over."

A peace fell over Anna Marie.

✍

That night after Sally tucked them safely into bed, both sisters lay quiet. Finally Louann spoke. "I miss Mama."

"Do you want a story?" Anna Marie whispered.

"Yes, please."

"When you were a baby, Daddy threw you above his head, and you threw up in his face."

Louann giggled. "What did he do?"

"He just laughed, but he put you down real quick. Mama told him he got what he deserved because throwing a baby around wasn't safe." The mention of Mama caused an ache in Anna Marie's ribs.

"Sally looks kind of like him. When she frowns, her forehead wrinkles up like Daddy's."

"Yes, you're right." Shame washed through Anna Marie for forgetting another of Daddy's important traits. "Sometimes I dream he's talking to me at night." She looked around the dark room and felt comforted. "Sally would never tell us if this was Daddy's room when he was little."

"She is hurt that he never came home with Mama and us. Maybe she thinks he was ashamed of his life here." Louann let out a loud yawn.

"Did Sally tell you that?" Anna Marie yawned too.

"No, I just know."

The hum of the night noises slipped into the cracked windows. The air was hot for March. Sally had said not to be surprised if another storm rolled in.

"It's weird for you to be thinking that up by yourself."

"Sometimes I just know things, Anna Marie." Louann's words floated on the night air, prickling the hairs on the back of her sister's neck.

"How do you know?" The hot air moved through the open window.

"I don't know how. It's like walking around in a dream. I see or hear something weird that doesn't make a bit of sense until later."

"If that happened to me I'd be scared."

"I told Mama about the dreams. She said not to worry, that I got this from Daddy. It's another reason he doesn't like this mountain."

Jealously punched Anna Marie in the stomach. Mama had told Louann a real secret. That wasn't fair. "Just go to sleep. We have to go to school in the morning." Her words had a harsher tone than she meant.

❦

The wind howled like an angry wolf, shaking the window-panes.

"Girls, get down here right now. We're going to the cellar." Daddy's voice rang in the room.

Was Anna Marie dreaming? The floorboards were smooth and kept her steps quiet. "Louann, get up. We have to go to the storm cellar."

Louann obeyed, following Anna Marie. Neither girl had shoes, but Anna Marie headed to the door. The roar of what sounded like a train filled the room.

"Run, Louann." The pure animal instinct to be safe pushed Anna Marie out the bedroom door and down the stairs. At the bottom a wail sounded. "Louann? Where are you?"

"What's going on?" Sally came out of her room in a man's robe belted at the waist.

"Another bad storm." The sound of splitting wood filled the space. The front door blew open and glass shattered in another room.

"Where is Louann?"

"She was right behind me." A wild cry trapped itself in Anna Marie's chest.

A loud crash shook the house. All went silent.

"Come on, girl." Sally ran up the stairs.

A huge oak tree stretched across the hall.

"Louann?" Anna Marie's scream came out like she was a wild animal in trouble. The hall was gone, caved in on itself.

"Girl, get yourself together. No time for this stuff. We got to get Louann out of the room." Sally ran her fingers through her hair.

Louann's nightgown stuck out from under the tree's massive trunk.

"You're small enough," Sally said. "Can you crawl in there and get your sister?"

"Yes ma'am." Anna Marie's gown ripped on a limb. A large gap in the floor almost pulled her inside.

"Hurry, child. This whole part of the house could go down with another gust of wind."

A large limb pressed into her stomach. The gap yawned wide. Anna Marie worked her arm around the limb and touched Louann's warm hand. "Can you crawl?"

"My other arm is stuck."

Part of the tree pinned Louann's arm to the mattress. The stars twinkled where the roof had once covered the room. Lightning flickered in the distance. "Here. I'm going to push down on the mattress and you pull your arm out. Do it quick, even if it hurts."

"Ok." Louann's tangled mess of hair covered one eye.

The mattress gave with ease, creating a slice of space.

Louann stood, her arm free but twisted at a wrong angle.

"Come on girls. Hurry," Sally fussed from the door. "We have to get out of this house."

Louann's good hand squeezed Anna Marie's fingers. "Watch the hole," Anna Marie said. "Get on your knees and follow me out. Don't use that arm."

Sally frowned when Anna Marie and Louann stood in front of her. "Your arm?"

"Yes ma'am. It doesn't hurt, though," Louann answered.

"From the looks of it, child, it should. Let's go. We'll have to head to the hospital when the wind dies down."

"I saw Daddy," Louann said. "He was here. He told me I was going to be fine and not to be scared."

A tiny cry escaped Sally. "You seen your daddy?" A look floated between Sally and Anna Marie, an understanding. "Folks always look after the ones they love, no matter what. Now come on."

≈

Louann's arm was badly broken in three places, and she spent five days in the hospital in Asheville. Her sister and grandmother stayed with one of Sally's friends, who didn't live far from the hospital, so they could visit every day.

When Louann was finally discharged and Sally took them home, a neighbor met her on the porch. "Hal brought this mail up the mountain to you. Said it looked important. I told him you were at the hospital."

Anna Marie watched Sally's face as she read it. "Girls, we got to go call your mama."

"Why? What's wrong?"

Sally gave Anna Marie a long look. "I ain't going to lie to you. Your daddy died two weeks ago in France."

Anna Marie looked at Louann. How could this happen?

"That means Daddy come from heaven to help us, Anna Marie. He was there watching over us."

"He'll always be with you two," Sally said in a broken voice. She looked older, tired.

๛

Anna Marie stayed on with Sally long after Daddy's body was shipped home and buried in the big cemetery on Black Mountain. Mama begged her to come with her to the new home she had made in Atlanta.

"I can't leave Sally, Mama. She needs me. You take Louann. I'll be right here. Daddy would want it that way."

Atlanta, 1986

"Look who we have." Doug stood behind my wheelchair. He had his own story about Grandma Anna. It seemed that she had come to him in a dream, telling him to get home as quick as he could drive. He couldn't sleep, tossing and turning. Finally, he decided to head home just to check on us.

In front of me was the window looking into the neonatal nursery. "See them. Three little boys in the bed together. Lord, don't you know they will be a handful when they get older? They're all breathing on their own."

Tubes ran into their tiny bodies. Fear and relief and adoration braided together to form pure love. "Are they okay?" I asked.

"The doctor said they're the healthiest triplets he's ever seen. They are thriving, was his words."

Thriving. The word rolled around inside of me. A strong word that made me think of Grandma Anna waving from the Burger King, waving me into the parking lot. No one knew what the world held for anyone, but I could move forward and make the best kind of life for my kids.

"Your mom wants you to call as soon as you can."

I looked at my baby boys. Beautiful, healthy boys. "I will." Mother would tell me what I already knew—that Grandma Anna had left the world—and I wasn't quite ready to hear the words. My three sons were side by side in the little bed. That's all I wanted for the moment.

WATERCOLOR SKY

1995

It seemed as if the wind was talking to me in raw and wicked whispers.—Pat Walker Johnson

The moon, round and full, made Alice Riley Parson think of daylight, defused and soft, settling on the snow, using the blanket of white to reflect what would have been a dull glow otherwise. A single broom-sage-colored rabbit hopped slow, cautious, looking here and there into the safety of the woods. The road unfolded up Black Mountain, and the twinkling stars in the black winter sky distracted Alice. She'd come here for a place to paint and be quiet. No children to ferry to different functions. No dinners to make her three sons and husband turn up their noses. No conversations, TV programs, phone calls, or newspaper. Time with crystal-clear stillness. Yes. Time that belonged only to her. The date was December 21. No, the car clock read 12:45 pm. December 22, Winter Solstice. A shiver ran through her cold bones, death passing over her future grave.

That morning had been off balance. Her postive attitude fell apart at breakfast with fighting children and Anthony, her husband, telling her to control the boys, as if these walking/talking genes of his weren't his at all. Alice bit her lip, and the coppery taste of blood shocked her. Later, Anthony went to the office to clear out paperwork before leaving for the holidays. The boys were scattered at friends' houses for one last visit before Christmas. The house was quiet, silent, yawning open with the promise of more chaos to come, and what felt like dread bubbled in Alice's chest. Complete dread that dug deep into her heart.

Christmas cookies might be nice. Flour, butter, water, eggs mixed into a thick dough and wrapped in wax paper, placed on the refrigerator's second shelf. She'd last seen her grandmother's Christmas cookie cutters in the storage closet. When the old sketchpad fell from the top shelf, fell open to a drawing of Gran's house, her garden, Alice packed an over-night bag with art supplies and dressed in a warm sweater— her favorite brown sweater that Anthony thought hideous— soft, worn jeans, and hiking boots. The car's full tank of gas gave Alice the excuse to slam the door behind her.

∽

The spruces, tall and straight sentries standing guard in the milky moonlight, opened the door to her childhood memo-ries. Roaming Black Mountain, free as any wild child could be. Strong women were missing from her family. Well, that wasn't exactly true. Gran, dull as a door, had shown strength just living alone on Black Mountain for years, without a man to guide her life. How fortunate Alice was to have Anthony to take care of the hard stuff. And the repayment he received was a missing wife close to Christmas.

The car knocked and sputtered while cold dread spread through her bones again. The engine died, and the car rolled to a stop. How could this happen? No houses in sight. The nearest one over two miles up the mountain. What had she been thinking? Leaving the comfort of her warm home? De-serting her half-grown boys? Anger rushed through her chest. At who or what, she wasn't sure. She only knew this was punishment for believing she could walk away on her own, imploding her safe life. The silent dark wrapped around the car. Cold seeped into her feet. If she died in the car on the lonely mountain road, would Anthony ever know? Her boys? The whole silly thought wasted her time. The icy wind hit her with full force when she opened the door.

Clouds raced across the moon without her noticing. Snowflakes rained, catching in her hair and eyelashes. She opened her mouth to the sky. The wet treat melted on her tongue. If she died in that minute, her headstone would read "A Lover Of Snow."

Back in the car, the cold was less. She could always layer the rest of her clothes and start walking. The sound of an engine rushed from behind, headlights moving toward her. The truck rattled so loud, she was sure at any minute it would fall to pieces. A figure climbed from the driver's side. A face appeared in the fogged window. The woman rapped on the glass.

"You okay in there?"

"I'm fine. My car isn't so good."

"You want to open that door so we can talk proper?"

The cold bit at Alice's fingers.

The woman wore a man's overcoat pulled tight around her. "Are you a traveler?" she asked.

"I guess I am." What a strange question.

"Come with me. It's too cold to spend the night here."

"I wouldn't want to bother you. The house I'm staying at is just up the mountain a ways."

"No bother. You're here to paint. It's my job to take you to a good place."

"How did you know I'm here to paint?"

"Let's go before the snow gets deeper."

"You could drop me at the house where I was going."

The woman's beautiful laugh tinkled like a wind chime. "Don't look this angel of mercy in the mouth. Are you coming or not?"

"Let me get my bag." Alice grabbed the bag of supplies from the back seat.

"I'm a weaver," the woman said as they moved toward her vehicle. "Maybe you would like my work."

"A weaver, how interesting. I'm sure I would love it."

"My mother and grandmother were both weavers." Alice noticed the lines on the woman's brown face, the wide gray swatch that streaked her black hair. Tiny colored beads hung from the knot of hair at the back of her neck. She kept step with the woman as if she were in a dream crossing the sky, entering solitude, a winter night.

"One of my great-grandmothers was full-blooded Cherokee," Alice said. "The family legend said she was a warrior in her own right, saving the land on this mountain from the government, saving her family from the Trail of Tears."

"Warrior is a strong name to give." The woman stopped and watched Alice. "Get into the truck."

The road was rough. Alice's car became smaller in the side mirror. As the truck flew up the rutted road, Alice half believed it would leave the ground and fly. Outside the window, the sky turned a soft midnight blue with streaks of green and pink. Too far south for northern lights. Instead of fear, Alice was wrapped in peace. She itched to use her paintbrush, splash watercolors on a canvas. The truck stopped with a hard thump. Alice fell forward as if she had been kicked from bed during a beautiful dream.

"Here we are."

The sky showcased the stars again, and moonlight

splashed on a cabin with smoke curling from the chimney. "This is my home, as it was my mother's and her mother's."

"Wonderful." And Alice couldn't have been more sincere.

"Hmph." The woman entered the home with Alice following behind.

The room was sparsely furnished but warmed by the blazing fire in the center fireplace. The woman sat in front of a large loom and began to work the rust-colored thread through the many vertical threads, reminding Alice of the potholders she had made as a child at camp. In and out, the rhythm lulled and soothed.

"Now it's your turn." The woman stood.

"I can't do that. I'm not a weaver. I'm not even an artist anymore. I'm nobody, only what others see."

"Come." The word was a soft command.

"Here." The woman pointed to the stool. The touch of her hand tingled on Alice's skin. "In and out, up and down. That is all. When you reach the end, push down. This is to tighten the pattern."

Alice settled in front of the loom. With each motion, a tune, strong, sweet, and soft, filled her mind. Towering spruces loomed above her. Horses, wild and running, men with strong bodies, women with muscles like men, babies hanging on their mothers' chests. She could smell the fresh, clear air of some placed existing before her.

The woman stood behind her as the sky became gray with morning light. Alice's hand worked in and out at a pace that amazed her. She caught the tender place of her life by its comet tail.

The woman bent close to Alice. "I am the warrior you

spoke of, the woman of strength. Paint. Use the gift bestowed on you, dear daughter."

Alice woke to the bitter cold and frozen fog on the inside of her car windows. Her hands and knuckles throbbed. She opened the door and witnessed the spruces scrubbing away at a pink sky to the east. She pulled her sketchbook from the back seat. Her charcoal pencil moved with the skill of a weaver. When she finished, the woman at her loom was captured on paper. This would be Alice's first oil painting. Thoughts beat inside her mind like the wings of a hawk as what she had come to find showed itself in a much different way.

She pulled a clean sheet of paper from her pad. On it she wrote, *I met my third great-grandmother, Polly Riley. She taught me who I am. I'm going home for awhile but not forever. I'm going home to paint and teach my boys about their strong grandmothers. I am a warrior. I finally believe in something I never believed in before. Myself.*

When she got into Asheville, the sun rode high. She stopped at the post office and mailed what she wrote to Anthony. Of course, she would reach home before the letter, but still he would learn how she felt and what she thought. If he read it. If he cared.

But nothing he said would spoil this new knowledge of her warrior self.

GHOST DOG

2019

The March wind undid several years of work getting a cattle farm started, did severe damage to our house, and put a fear of tornado winds in me that lasted for years.
—Robert Hollis

"Mom, that dog is back under the tree," Davie yelled as he crashed through the door with all his boy-turning-man masculine energy. All arms and legs at thirteen.

"Don't go near the poor thing." The tall window in the back room of the house framed the large oak and the mountain just beyond. Black Mountain. It was on fire with orange and red leaves, even though the temperature suggested summer. The dog sat under our colorful tree.

"Helicopter mom," Davie complained.

"Yes, that's me." The sandy-colored dog looked tired, too skinny, and pretty much a mongrel someone had tried to let out in the "country." "I think something is wrong with him."

The dog turned and stared in the window, at me, as if he could hear my words.

"He's hungry." Davie scooped a fistful of chocolate out of the candy dish that sat on my desk.

"I put food out there yesterday, but he never ate it."

"See? You want him too." When Davie laughed, I had to look away. Jamie's face lit up on our son.

"I confess, I'm a sucker." The dog looked toward the mountain. "The poor thing looks pitiful, like he's lost his best friend. I don't understand people dumping dogs off somewhere."

"Yesterday when I rode my bike up the drive, I thought I saw someone standing under the tree."

"Who?" I tried to keep fear out of my voice.

He shrugged. "I just saw them for a second and the driveway dipped, keeping me from seeing the tree. When I came up the hill, only the dog sat there."

"No one should have been in the yard."

"I told you no one was there. I just thought I saw someone. They couldn't get out of sight that quick, Mom." His emphasis on "Mom" let me know what he was thinking before he voiced the thought. "We moved here in the middle of nowhere so we could have a new life, a safer life, remember?"

And he was right. We came here for a fresh start. "I know. This place is so much better than the city, but you know how I love a mystery. You don't imagine things. You had to see something." I glanced out again. The dog was gone. That quick.

"I'm going over to Peter's." Davie darted through the back door.

"Hey."

"I know. I'll be in way before dark. I won't talk to anyone I don't know. That means I can barely speak to anyone." He was out the door before I could stop him.

"Before dark!" I yelled from the back porch.

"Yeah, okay Mom."

Sweat broke out on my forehead. Crazy how cool the old house stayed. The fourteen-foot ceilings made it feel like central air was running. Parts of the house were pre-Civil War. At one point, over a thousand acres went with the place. It was a fully functional farm for years and owned by the same family until we moved in a few months before, but by then only five acres remained. The back porch was used as a potting shed by the old woman who owned the house until she died. My sister—she bought the house for Davie and me after Jamie died—said the woman had been a famous gardener. Her roses were known all over the country, and stories appeared in papers and magazines throughout the South. In the overgrown garden, one perfect rose bloomed on a skinny bush. Did roses usually bloom in fall?

A flash of blue moved near the old oak tree, but nothing was there. Maybe a blue jay? The place was filled with wildlife. My cup ran over with peace and quiet. Just what my doctor ordered.

"Murray." A woman's voice caught in the hot, sticky wind. The sound in the valley carried. Sometimes I heard the neighbors talking on their porch a good three acres away.

Upon meeting the couple, and of course being my unfiltered self, I told them I could hear them from my place.

The husband laughed. "This valley has borrowed magic from Black Mountain."

Magic. What a childish but delicious idea. What would I do with magic? The woman's call did not sound again. Murray must have gone home. Two steps from the tree, a child's voice sounded.

"Murray, come home." Again the woman's call. The shade of the tree gave me a moment of stillness, and warmth spread through me. The child would follow his mother's call. Don't children always come when mothers call?

Past, 1940

The soaring bird, a hawk, skimmed the tops of the trees as if he were searching for his hiding prey, searching like the rest of us. The boy, age two, had wandered the mountain for two days and counting. Every able-bodied person combed the area. The hawk beat his wings, using keen senses and sight and striking like a lightning bolt, disappearing behind the treetops and returning as a dark shadow against a dull slate sky. It was March, the month that couldn't be trusted. One day summer-like, the next winter. When the hawk reached the highest point, the place where he almost seemed to pause, his body became a bullet and shot down, summoning speed, propelling straight at the ground. Instincts. Survival. This time talons opened. A tiny brown and white wren caught in his deadly grip as he swung his flight level. His cry washed over the mountain, echoing through the valley. Those of us searching stopped and watched the hawk fly across the field, prey held tightly.

"Murray, come home," yelled the mother, who wore a bright blue dress so maybe her son would see her, find his way home.

Present, 2019

The night air seeped in the windows, cool and delicious as fall should be. Fat pillows cushioned my back against the high antique wooden headboard. I owed my comfort to my sister, Kathy. Every Sunday we met somewhere for lunch, her treat, and a long talk. We'd never seen each other when Jamie was alive outside of the occasional holiday. I was her project. A little sister who needed molding, rebirthing. She

probed me to get back to photography. I had my own flour-
ishing business in Atlanta and had been recognized for my
success until Jamie was killed in a plane accident. Fear overtook me, and I retreated from my life, trying to take Davie
with me.

"You have PTSD, sis. You have to get out. Start living
again."

This was so easy for Kathy to say. No one had been
snatched from her. She lived in her artist bubble, where she
thought she was untouchable.

"Come to Asheville to photograph," she urged.

"Yes, I should."

My camera still held photos of Jamie. The thought of
looking at them was horrible, and even worse was the
thought of removing them. My whole self was stuck inside
some in-between world.

Jamie's plane went down not too far from Asheville,
deep in the mountains. I hated that plane, hated that he insisted flying himself on business trips instead of using the
ticket his company would provide. A search party of fifty
men, professional trackers, combed the area where the plane
dropped. On the third day they found the wreckage but no
Jamie. There were signs he had crawled away, searching for
help. His blood-covered seat promised he couldn't have gotten far. *Lost* was a huge, heavy word. Maybe a bear found
him? Such thoughts often tried to invade. Two years had
passed, and his body was never found.

Kathy assured me I had every right to be afraid. Who
wouldn't be?

Yes, this cozy room with the fireplace and large windows must have been the master bedroom where the woman
lived and maybe died. She was in her nineties. A long life. A

well-to-do family. A woman who outlived her children—if she had any—and her husband. She probably had a good life free of the gut-wrenching fear I lived with all the time.

A shadow of a person stood in the corner of the room, close to one of the windows. The fuzzy form grew sharper. A flash of blue. Maybe a dress. A woman?

I blinked and the shadow was gone.

"I'm losing my mind. I really have to get out of this house. Start taking photos. I have to do it." My words bounced off the high ceilings.

"Mom, are you talking to someone?" Davie called from his room down the hall.

"Get to sleep. It's 10:30. You have school tomorrow."

"All my friends stay up to 11:00."

"They are not my children. Sleep. Now."

"Ok."

"Davie, I think I'll go take some photos tomorrow after you leave for school."

"Sure, Mom. Sounds good."

The silence filled the space between our rooms.

Past, 1940

"Murray, stay under the big tree with Dickie."

The scruff of a dog followed the little boy everywhere. Dickie was better about watching the little boy than his parents. My mama would grab her chest at the thought of a two-year-old left to roam a big farm with only a dog. When I was young, she watched me like a hawk. Just thinking about her made my stomach turn hard as a rock. Missing your family wasn't a dang bit of fun.

"Letter, Landon." Will slapped the crinkled brownish

envelope to my chest. Like me, he was in the CCC (Civil Conservation Corps). We were there in North Carolina from Georgia. Our group was assigned to Black Mountain to work on Mr. William Shaw's farm. Three decent-size meals a day were a regular occurrence. My pay, five dollars a week, was mailed to Mama and Daddy for help in feeding the rest of the family. The Depression killed off livelihoods everywhere—mill workers, domestics, and sharecroppers like Daddy. Once upon a time, we had our own farm that kept all of us fed and dressed well. Once upon a time, life was good even if we had to work hard. Then the storm hit with a wind that destroyed the barn, killing three cows, our meat and milk for the winter. Daddy couldn't make his loan payment and the bank foreclosed. We sharecropped for a man who was meaner than any sin a man could commit. Even took a portion of our kitchen garden.

Watching the great Mr. William Shaw strut around this farm with a suit and tie, his shoes shiny, made my head roar. The look he gave us CCC guys told the whole story. He was better than any of us. Never in his life had he got greasy from working on his tractor. No sir, he had a man to do that for him. At least Mrs. Shaw was a real nice woman, like Mama, except much younger. Anyone could tell she came from a working life, maybe even a hard life. She ran that two-thousand-acre farm with a determined strength none of us guys could criticize.

"Boy, read letters on your own time. We got fields to turn today," the boss, Mr. Macon, barked at me.

"I'm helping set up the lunch tables, sir, for Mrs. Shaw." President Roosevelt was a real stickler on us CCC boys eating on time. We weren't slaves to people like Mr. Macon.

"Then get to helping and stop standing around." He

crossed the lawn to speak with Mr. Shaw, whose eyes were already glassy with liquor. This was the reason Mrs. Betty Shaw, pretty and younger than Mr. Shaw, did all the decision making. We boys knew to bring her any questions about work. She had urged me over and over to call her Betty, but the whole thing wasn't proper.

"Hand over here," Bill called from the picnic tables set off to the side of the house. "Mrs. Shaw wants the tables in the shade because it's so hot. Storm headed our way. I can feel it." He sniffed the air. "Smells like my mama's meatloaf today."

Little Murray was under the massive tree, playing with what looked like tin soldiers. Dickie sat nearby, the guard.

"Shade is hot today," I said. "I love meatloaf. Hope she makes that cornbread. I love that stuff."

As Bill and me placed the fourth table under the tree, Murray walked away, Dickie tagging along.

"The kid is wandering off." I let my end of the heavy table drop.

Bill studied the small figure heading toward the field. The mountain hovered in the distance. He shrugged. "You go tell Mr. Shaw." He nodded. "He thinks we don't have no sense. Go on over there. He can see the boy with his own two eyes. It's best to be seen and not heard."

"Yeah, the kid does go everywhere by himself."

"He ain't alone. He's got that old dog. He'd take a hand off if someone touched the boy." Bill laughed.

"You're probably right."

Murray disappeared from sight.

Present, 2019

"I wish you would let me give you a ride to school, Davie." I said this even though I didn't really mean it. The Russian tea was perfect, and I didn't want to put it down. "The weather is supposed to get bad today."

"Mom, quit treating me like I'll disappear or die. If the storms come, you can pick me up from school. It's sunny this morning. I like to catch the bus with the guys."

The sun streaked across the old wooden floors of my workroom. "Ok. I'm going to hike and take some photos. I need to get back to work."

"That's good, Mom. Maybe you can sell some to magazines. Get your old clients back." He shoveled the maple-flavored oatmeal into his mouth.

"Thanks for the vote of confidence."

"It's tough living with an old woman, retired from her job. She's too bored."

I threw the wet dishcloth at him, nailing him in the shoulder.

He swiped it away. "That's nasty, Mom."

"Don't mess with this old woman."

He pushed his chair back.

"Brush your teeth before you leave."

"Mom."

"Don't Mom me."

His shoulders slumped. "Ok."

After Davie was on the bus, I set out through the field, my camera hanging around my neck. The broom sage was up to my waist in places. Beggar lice clung to my jeans. The mountain seemed close from the patio, but it was much farther away. From this distance and through the camera, the house stood stately and elegant, in contrast to the old and forgotten feel that existed inside. Click, click, click. Photo after photo.

The mountain became bigger and bigger, looming in its own dark shadow. The sheer mass threatened to swallow me, hide me away from the reality of my life.

Past, 1940

"Murray." Mrs. Shaw's voice was strained, tight.

By then the tables sat grouped under the huge oak tree's shade. Mrs. Shaw's call caught up with me in the field where some of us were raking rocks after the plow passed by.

"Murray, where are you?" She didn't talk to any of us.

I had moved closer to the base of the mountain when I saw the foreman walking his horse up and down the rows, pausing to speak. When he stopped in front of me, dread spread through my bones.

"Have you see the boy? Has he come this way?"

The opportunity to tell the whole truth lay before me. The words stuck in my chest. "Haven't seen him since he was under the tree. I was helping with the tables." This was the truth with a few details left out.

"If you see anything, yell."

"Ok."

He moved on to the next guy.

By the time we got word that folks were forming a search party, more than two hours had passed since the boy and dog left the safety of the tree. The sun hung straight up in the sky.

Sweat ran from the top of my head into my eyes as fifty of us CCC guys met at the tables. A good-size group of local

88

farmers milled around. The law had brought the other part of our group, who were working on the Swannanoa River, making a crowd of around a hundred. Mrs. Shaw stood under the tree, twisting her apron.

"Murray Shaw is missing," the sheriff announced. "He's two years old and may have a dog with him. If any of you seen anything, talk to me. We're going to make a line across the field and walk. Look at the ground. If you see anything unusual, stop and raise your hand. Anything at all. What is he wearing, Mrs. Shaw?" He turned to look at her.

"Short tan pants and a blue button-up shirt. He's wearing his oxfords with blue socks." Her voice, smooth and in control, eased the fear in my stomach.

"Ok. Let's go." The sheriff waved his hand.

Mrs. Shaw walked with the row in front of me.

"Don't you want to stay here with your husband in case the boy comes home?" The sheriff touched her elbow.

The slight pixie of a woman stopped in her tracks. Her row of men and my row stopped too, as if she was leading us. "Would you, Sheriff Turner? If your boy was lost, would you?"

"I'll wait here and watch for Murray," Mr. Shaw called out, standing behind the rows. "Betty needs to go."

We walked toward the mountain. The boy couldn't have gone that far. No way he made it far up the mountain. The field stretched in front of us. Most of it had been turned over with the plow earlier that morning. If the boy was around, he could be seen. The locals insisted Black Mountain was magic. I didn't believe a bit in magic. Clouds built behind us. Piled high on top of each other. Black and gray. Headed in the direction of the mountain.

Present, 2019

The sun heated the earth like it was a July day in Atlanta. Only I was in Western North Carolina, where the air was crisp and cool in late October. The suffocating heat disappeared when I stepped into the trees and began climbing the mountain. The clouds in the western sky piled high with blue-gray tops, promising thunderstorms. Still, they were in the far distance. Birds of all kinds flitted and called through the trees. Squirrels chattered as they jumped from one branch to another. Chipmunks scampered here and there. Above me gold, yellow, and red leaves with a slash of orange provided a canopy. The ground was covered with a soft bed of pine straw and bright green moss. A dead log ran across the path.

A flash of blue caught my attention ahead. Maybe an Eastern bluebird. The temperatures dropped the deeper I walked into the woods. Large outcroppings of boulders towered above me. Water trickled down their sides as if they wept. At the top of the hill, a patch of blue flirted with the darkness of the tree trunks and disappeared. A sharp breezed moved through the treetops. At the top of the steep incline, the view opened. The sky, still clear, showed me the blue I had caught a glimpse of while climbing. The patches of clouds had moved closer. The big tree in the backyard below shielded my view of most of the house, but I caught a glance of the garden, the dot of the single red rose. And there was the dog, walking to the base of the tree. His movements were old and tired. I snapped several shots.

"Murray, where are you? There is a storm moving in, dear. Time to come home. Dickie?"

The dog under the tree perked up his ears, as if he too

was listening to the woman. She needed to keep up with the child. If he was young enough not to be in school, he shouldn't be allowed to roam the area alone. The sound of pebbles bouncing off other rocks behind me drew my attention. A dog, not so different from the stray, stood on top of a flat rock. He let out a howl. Out of pure instinct, I snapped a photo instead of leaving.

"What are doing? Are you looking for Murray and Dickie?"

The dog watched me with dark eyes. Then, he walked away. Again the woman's voice called. Two missing boys. Should I find her? Help her search for these children she had lost?

Past, 1940
Newspaper Article

One of the worst possible problems fell upon the search party hunting for the two-year-old Shaw boy, lost earlier this morning when he wandered away from his house while his mother, Mrs. Betty Shaw, prepared dinner for the CCC boys that work on her husband's farm. She was positive Murray had been under the big oak tree in her backyard only minutes before she noticed him missing. A search party was formed with the CCC boys and local farmers. They were combing the area when a storm with tornado winds hit the valley. Surrounding farms and houses sustained extensive damage. A tractor near the Shaw house was flipped upside down. Searchers scattered for cover. Mrs. Shaw had to be forced by Sheriff Turner to retreat. The whole town of Swannanoa Gap are praying for Murray Shaw and his dog, Dickie, who was said to be quite a protector, following the boy everywhere, even sleeping on his bed at night. Mr. William Shaw, the boy's father and leader in Swannanoa Gap, says the dog just showed up one day in the yard under the tree, and his son fell in love with him. That was well over a year ago.

If anyone sees a young boy around two with blond wispy hair, you should keep him and find a deputy. His parents are sure Murray is only lost, maybe on Black Mountain, not far from their farm. You folks up there keep a look out for him too.

Present, 2019

The air was thick with humidity by the time I got back to the house. My workroom had the best natural light. The photos on my camera's SD card flashed on the computer screen. I was careful not to go too far back through the files in fear I would get a glimpse of Jamie. One of the new photos caught my attention. One of the house. Maybe sellable. When I zoomed in on the second story, a woman stood at a window, staring into the yard. There was no mistaking it. The image, clear and sharp, was the profile of a woman, her hair cropped close to her head. It wasn't just my eyes this time. The image was captured.

I called Kathy.

"Hello?"

"I have a question for you."

"What is it?"

"Who was the old lady who lived here?"

Kathy gave a little laugh. "Why are you asking about her?"

"Just curious. A lot of this furniture has to be hers."

"Her name was Betty Shaw. She outlived her whole family, including her husband, William Shaw, who was some big deal in his time. At one time the Shaw farm was over two thousand acres. Lots of history. She died two years ago. I bought the house right after it went on the market. I thought I'd live there and work on my art, but it was too far away, too removed from the art scene in Asheville. You haven't seen anything, have you?"

"Seen what? I don't know what you mean."

"There are rumors that Betty walks in her garden." Kathy's voice held a tease of a laugh.

"I was out taking photos and it got me thinking about the history."

"Oh wonderful, Sarah. I'm so excited."

"Yes, it felt good."

"Bring your photos to lunch on Sunday."

"How did you know Betty Shaw?"

"She was interested in one of my paintings and paid a ridiculous amount."

"What painting?"

"One of Davie when he was two, playing in that field close to Dad's house. Remember? Betty loved it. Said it reminded her of someone in her family."

"Is the painting here?"

"I don't know. Look through the house. Anything you find in that house is yours. Rummage away. I have to run. See you Sunday."

"Thanks. See you then." I ended the call.

The day had turned gray in that short time. I went upstairs, switching on lights as I went. Clearing out the hall linen closet had been a goal of mine since moving in. The top shelf was crammed with old boxes and books. Faded cotton linens were folded on the rest of the shelves. On the bottom shelf was the painting, covered with a towel. Davie flying a kite with Jamie. The day I took the photo Kathy used had been windy, with white fluffy clouds racing across the sky. Jamie had showed Davie how to hold the kite string and guide it, a big deal for a two-year-old. Kathy's use of the photo spun a horde of feelings, each with a descriptive word. Love, contentment, grace. I decided to hang the painting in my workroom. A large book crashed to the floor from the top shelf. An old scrapbook with a newspaper article glued to one of the brown pages.

Past, 1940

Newspaper Article

Missing Boy's Body Found

The body of little Murray Shaw was found today after three days of searching. Landon Parker, one of the young men from the CCC who helped search, found the boy facedown on the steep side of Black Mountain. There were no visible marks of physical violence, indicating the boy died from exposure to what surely was a tornado only hours after his disappearance.

The body was not moved pending the arrival of the county coroner from Asheville. Mr. William Shaw, prominent farmer, was devastated beyond words by the news. The thirty-year-old mother, Betty Shaw, who had been on the verge of a breakdown, seemed slightly relieved.

"At least I know what happened to him. I couldn't stand not ever knowing."

The boy's dog was found near the body and would not allow Landon Parker to touch the child. The deputies were deeply saddened when they were forced to kill the dog so they could examine the child. Landon Parker broke down when the dog was killed and had to be carried off the mountain.

Present, 2019

When Davie stepped off the bus that afternoon, the wind was much stronger. "Mom, I'm starving."

"How about homemade cookies?" I asked with a laugh.

"Yes!" He ran into the house.

I followed him inside and glanced into my workroom close to the kitchen. Kathy's painting hung over my desk. The scrapbook sat open on the overstuffed chair. "Cookies are in the pantry unless you'd like healthy fruit."

"Cookies. Can I take these to share with the guys?" he called.

"Come look at this." I straightened the frame of the painting.

"Wow. Did Aunt Kathy paint that?"

"Yes, she did. You were two. You won't remember this."

"I do. Dad showed me how to fly the kite. It was the best day ever." His face lit up. "But where did you get the painting? Did Aunt Kathy bring it by?"

"No. The weird thing is your aunt met the woman who owned this house when she bought this painting at the gallery. I found it in the closest upstairs."

"Peter says this house is haunted." Davie took a big bite of his chocolate chip cookie.

"People make up stories about old houses and their owners."

"Peter swears he's seen a boy wandering at the edge of the woods near the mountain. He's crazy. Right Mom?"

"He just likes ghost stories." I ruffled his hair.

"I don't believe in ghosts. If they were real, Dad would have come back to see me." The look on his face betrayed his hope.

"Dad is at peace. He wouldn't come looking for us. Ghosts are not at peace."

He shrugged. "I'm going to Peter's."

I looked out and saw the dog standing under the tree. The sky was gray, but I saw no rain or angry clouds. "What are you guys doing at Peter's?"

"We're going over to Jake's house today. It's at the bottom of Black Mountain. I'll be home on time."

"Be home before dark."

He shot out of the room, extra cookies in tow. I followed to watch him leave. He rode his bike down the drive, swishing by me. "Be careful," I called out.

A set of comfortable chairs would be perfect under the tree. The packed dirt was solid. Brick pavers would create a patio. Something stuck out of the ground, small and metal. Water had washed down from the field and over the roots of the tree, wearing away the topsoil. It was a toy, a tin soldier. Old. Some faded, almost undetectable blue paint still marked the uniform. I shoved it down in my jeans pocket and headed back to the house to take a look at the scrapbook.

A dark line of clouds balanced on the tree line far in the west. The rain and storms were headed our way, but Davie would be home before they arrived. I had to stop being a helicopter mom.

Past, 1940

The storm came out of nowhere that afternoon. One minute the sun hung in the sky, and the next a long black cloud moved over and dropped pure hell on us. The storm looked like the one that hit my family's farm and destroyed our lives. The birds stopped singing, and the air was still. I could hear the guy next to me breathing. But I kept searching for Murray. He should have been found by then. One guy said maybe he was kidnapped. This was silly, but then he didn't know what I knew—that Murray had simply walked away with his dog following.

"That boy is alive on the mountain, in the woods, probably scared to death, calling for his mama, and ain't nobody finding him," I said. "We need to quit making up stories and find him and that stupid dog."

Bill had a long stick, stirring the brush. "I thought the dog was pretty smart."

"If he was smart, he would have brought the boy home. That boy's on the mountain. What boy wouldn't want to climb up there?"

Why had I listened to Bill earlier and kept quiet? The air turned thick as soup with a tinge of yellow. "Storm headed this way."

That's all I had time to say as the monster cloud moved toward us. Trees split in half or broke like matchsticks. I dropped to the ground in a dip. The whole thing lasted about three minutes but seemed like forever. When the storm stopped, I yelled. "Bill, are you there?"

"Here." Bill pushed up from the brush.

The rest of the searchers stood up, one by one.

"God, I hope that boy is safe." This left my mouth before I could pull the words back inside.

The search went on for another two days. Mr. Shaw had taken to standing in the yard, watching for his son. "This valley carries sound. If he cries out, I'll hear him." He refused to move from the backyard.

When rain began to fall in buckets again for the third time in two days, the sheriff came to talk to Mr. Shaw. "Your

97

son is in God's hands, William. We have to go in for now."

Mrs. Shaw walked past both of them with a blanket. "I'm going to have one more look at those rocks."

"It's too dangerous in the dark," Sheriff Turner called. She kept walking. One of the guys took her a lantern, and she sat on a big rock all night in the rain.

On the third morning, cold settled around the farm. Frost crunched under my boots as I moved up the steep trail on the mountain. This was our third time searching the area. Murray had to be somewhere. I noticed a path to the left of the well-worn one that I hadn't noticed before. The brush grew high on both sides, making movement slow. Mama always said going at a problem slowly could help solve it. As I rounded a corner and the steepest part of the trail climbed in front of me, I heard a rumbling growl and a bark. Dickie stood on a rock above me.

"Hey boy, are you ok? Where's Murray?" That's when I saw the blue shirt and brown shorts. The little boy's back was covered in dog hair. His face was down in the pine straw that covered the ground and rocks. Both of his shoes were on, but only one sock. He didn't move. I took one step forward, but Dickie jumped on the boy's back and barked as if he meant to attack me.

"I'm just here to help him."

The dog was having none of it.

"Is anyone around?" If I left, I might lose my way trying to come back to the spot. "Anyone there?" I yelled, cupping my hands around my mouth.

Dickie barked and growled.

"Where you at?" came a voice from far off.

"Off the path to the left near the rocks. I found him. Hurry."

When the men broke through the brush into the clearing, Dickie went crazy. "Is the boy breathing?"

"I can't tell. Can't get close enough."

"We have to get to him." One older man stepped forward, and Dickie latched onto his forearm with his teeth. The other man shot the dog with his rifle. The sound echoed through the valley, traveling news that told of death. Dickie died beside Murray. Mama always said the mind could only handle so much. And mine cracked open.

Present, 2019

The cover of the scrapbook was leather, nice leather. The first page was a handsome photo of a couple getting married. The bride—it must be Betty Shaw—wore a light-colored, tailored suit that matched her boyish small figure. The man was tall with dark hair, wearing a suit and tie. Both smiled, Betty more than her new husband. The next few pages were photos of what the house and fields looked like back then. Next came a pudgy baby in his mother's arms. The new father looked over her shoulder. Both smiled at their child. The name printed underneath was Murray Shaw. Oh my. Hadn't I heard the woman yelling for Murray to come home?

The next page was the boy's first birthday party, with balloons and a cake outside under the large tree. The following photos were of the boy, Murray, a little older. Beside him was a dog that looked almost the same as our stray. I thought of the toy in my pocket and dug it out. Was it Murray's The photos were surely from the late thirties or forties. How could a toy stay under a tree that long? The next photo was a group of young men, about fifty of them, all wearing what looked like military uniforms. Under it was written "CCC." These boys were working away from home to help their families and to eat decent meals.

I flipped the page and a sticky breeze blew over me. Several newspaper articles were glued to the pages. One headline sent a chill through my bones: "Storm Hits While Searching for Lost Boy." As if on cue, a howl of wind blew through the yard, swaying the oak tree.

"Find your boy." The voice was all around me. Real. Not in my head. "Find him now."

I ran to the door. The sky was a sickly green color. The dog stood beside me and barked at the mountain. "I'm taking the car up that mountain," I said to the dog.

He barked and ran toward the field.

"Hey, come here. You can ride with me." But the dog kept running. I jumped in the car and peeled out of the driveway. Davie had said his friend lived at the bottom of Black Mountain. I couldn't find a single driveway. Maybe this was the wrong place. The mountain base was big, and his friend's house could be farther up the road.

Suddenly, I saw the stray standing in the middle of the street. I slammed on the brakes. He ran down a drive to the right that was hidden by large, vine-covered tree branch. Some primal instinct that only mothers have kicked in, and I followed the dog. I honked the horn when the house came into view. I saw no bikes.

A woman came to the door.

"I'm looking for my son, Davie. Is he here? There's a tornado headed our way." And just as I said this, treetops began cracking.

"They were right here a minute ago." The woman wore a desperate expression.

A scream worked in my chest, but the dog ran around the back of the house. I followed him with the woman close behind. The dog ran up a steep embankment, stopped at the top to see if I was coming. The wind pulled at me, but I made it up the bank. The woman slid.

"Here." I held out my hand.

Her grip was strong and she pulled herself up. The dog barked from the path. I was right behind. Trees cracked close and I yelled, "Davie." The sound of the wind swallowed the name. I stood on a flat rock. Davie and two boys huddled under a rock ledge.

I ran under the ledge with the boys. The woman piled in too. Both of us used our bodies as shields. Scientists say that wind cannot be seen, but that day I saw the smoky white wind reaching out for anything in its path. The woman and I held fast to the children, becoming one in our common mission.

The storm stopped as suddenly as it had started. The boys were fine, if not somewhat humble to us mothers who had found them. "Where is our dog?" Davie asked.

As if he heard, the dog walked out of the trees and ran straight for Davie, licking his face.

"Wow, that's the ghost dog, Mom," Davie's friend said to his mother.

"It does seem that way." The woman smiled. "I'm Jewel Parker, and you are?"

"Sarah Greene. You know Davie." I laughed. Later Jewel Parker would become my dear friend, and we would visit each other often. She would tell me the story of her father-in-law, Landon Parker, the man who found the lost boy, dead, not far from where our boys took shelter. Killed by a storm just as bad as the one we lived through.

The dog jumped into our car with us as we headed home. Ghost or not, he was a living, breathing animal. He had saved my Davie's life. But if Betty Shaw hadn't called out to me, I might not have left in time. That night, and every night after, the dog slept in the house on Davie's bed. Davie named him Buster.

I watched Davie and the dog sleep, afraid to leave them alone. A shadow of a woman stood just outside the door. "Thank you, Betty," I whispered.

As long as Betty was on guard, another boy would not die in a storm on that mountain.

Past

Newspaper Articles

Tribute Paid to Murray Shaw
1940

Over 2,000 attempted to crowd the small Methodist church in Swannanoa Gap today for the service of William and Betty Shaw's son, Murray Shaw. The crowd was so large Sheriff Turner closed the road leading to the church and people lined each side to wait for the procession. The CCC boys were allowed to attend because they screached tirelessly over the three days before the two-year-old was found. Landon Parker was invited to sit with Mr. And Mrs. Shaw. Parker was the young man who found the body and broke down. He claimed the whole thing was his fault because he saw the boy and his dog walk away from the spot under the tree. No amount of convincing made Mr. Landon see this otherwise. He will, no doubt, be marked for life.

Shaw Farm Boasts Largest Rosebush
1955

Landon Parker, the Shaw Farm's head foreman, was honored today by the Swannanoa Gap Garden Club for growing the largest rosebush the county has on record. The opened roses are the size of a large man's fist. The thirty-five-year-old foreman posed for photos with the famous bush and gave all the credit to Betty Shaw, our famous gardener. He insisted she come and be part of the photos. Both are more than employer and employee. They are friends. Those familiar with her son's death some fifteen years ago know Betty Shaw can't be kept down. She is a woman to be reckoned with and stands tall in this town.

Part Two

A Little Removed

TAKE ME HOME

An Imagined Story of Georgia's Central State Hospital

1950

A huge oak tree, washstand, with #3 tubs and wash pots. My chore, fill the pots with water, build a fire under them. Monday was washday. When laundry was on the line, used first rinse tub water to scrub the outhouse, bathed in second. I still have one of the pots. —Robert Hollis

Granny Atkins drank her coffee from a saucer and took a good dip of Bruton of an evening.—Raymond Atkins

First Measure
Beat 1

A twelve-year-old's idea of a perfect June would not include leaving the mountains and going further south, into the broiling heat and humidity of Middle Georgia. But this is a story about place, freedom, and a ghost that died twice, maybe a million times, before she was buried. It's a story of how Mama broke away from a place where she would always be the washwoman for white ladies. In June 1950, Mama took my hand and we left our tiny house on the other side of the river in Swannanoa Gap. Walked away on that hot morning to the train depot. Mama snapped her change purse open and dug out money that was all quarters, nickels, and dimes. The white man running the ticket window gave her a strong look. "Where you going?"

"Home." Her words were firm, solid, not to be messed with.

"Where is home?"

"Milledgeville, Georgia."

"That's going to be twenty dollars round trip for one."

"No sir. I need two one-way tickets. We won't be coming back."

"Then it is still twenty." He frowned.

Mama counted out the money real slow like.

The man counted the money again before he gave us our tickets. "The colored car is in the back of the train."

Mama nodded and whispered to me. "Ain't it always?"

Beat 2

Mama sang everywhere, and the train was no different. Sometimes she'd forget herself and start singing loud. When we pulled into the Milledgeville depot, folks were tapping their feet and clapped when Mama stopped.

"Thank you." She looked at her feet.

The sun sat bright in the sky. An older woman stood on the platform and waved when she saw us. "Lordy, you two are the best things I've seen in a mighty long time." The woman was as round as she was tall. It's a wonder Mama didn't pop a lung when the woman hugged her. When she finished, she turned to me. "Get over here and hug your Granny Esther. It's a sin not to have seen you since you were bitty." Granny Esther closed in fast. The smell of honeysuckle perfume made me think of playing outside all day while Mama hung clothes on the line. "I'm so glad you're here, Emmaline. Bet no one has talked about me because of that no-good daddy of yours."

Mama cleared her throat.

"And look at you, Rachel Price. My heart is about to burst." Granny Esther didn't pay Mama's protest a bit of mind. Instead she dropped one of her arms to draw Mama in the embrace again. "My gals are here. God is good. We got us some eating to do." She looked at Mama. "Rachel, I got you a job at the hospital and the pay is decent." She looked at me. "You have to be the prettiest granddaughter a woman could have. But a little skinny. We got to work on that."

"The pay has to be good. That hospital ain't nothing but haunted." Mama gave me a side look. She did this anytime we was talking without words over Daddy's notice.

Beat 3

Granny Esther's house was white with green metal awnings over all the windows. The other houses on her road looked a lot like hers, just different colors.

"This is where I grew up," Mama said, turning to speak to me in the back seat when we pulled in. "I went to school just down the road."

The kitchen was a cheery yellow with wooden cabinets that shined from polish.

"I hope you're hungry, Emmaline. I got us some meat-loaf and fresh tomatoes."

"That sounds good." I glanced into the living room. There was a TV. We never had a TV at home, so the thought of watching one made my stomach flip over.

"Why don't you help your mama put your things away."

I found Mama in the bathroom hanging her robe on the

back of the door.

"Wow, look at that tub," I blurted.

Mama smiled. "I know, it looks like a tub that goes in some rich house. I can't wait to fill it up with bubbles and soak away."

"Me too."

"We're going to be happy here, Emmaline."

"I know." But I couldn't help thinking about Daddy, even though he could be meaner than a snake.

Beat 4

"How can a hospital be haunted?" I sat on the bed in a strange room where I would live. The living part I hadn't bargained for, but I did love the little vanity and the round mirror, where I could sit and brush out my hair. Of course I dearly hated anything to do with my hair. My head was so tender, all someone had to do was look at it and I hurt.

"Well, lots of dying goes on in a hospital, but this one is not a regular hospital. It's been around since before slaves were freed. It's a place you get sent when you don't fit in with what is normal. Lots of women and black folks are there for no good reason."

"Why?"

"The world is a crazy, unfair place, Emmaline. Some of us folks have targets on us just because we are who we are or we get in the way or we're born with something not quite the same as the rest of people."

Mama pulled the lace curtains over the windows, leaving them open to the night air. "Enough talk." She gave me a rare hug. Don't get me wrong; she loved me, but hugs didn't come natural to her.

"Is Daddy okay?" The humming of heat bugs ate the silence between us.

"Don't you worry about your daddy. Anything that is wrong with him was brought on by his own doing, not mine. I've always wanted to put him six feet under."

I pulled the clean, crisp sheet up to my neck, even though the sticky hot was dipping around me.

"Go to sleep."

"Where will I stay while you're at work?"

Mama stopped at the door. "Your granny will watch you. I have the evening shift, three to eleven. You two can get to know each other."

Second Measure
Beat 1

A creak on the floor or a rattling in the ceiling must have woke me from a deep sleep. The lace curtains moved in a stale breeze. A mournful sound, maybe some night bird, eased into the room like a ghost floating above the bed. At first I thought Mama was singing some real sad song.

Take me home. I need to go home. My name is Lina Hunter. Come help me.

The voice echoed through the pecan grove out back, squeezing close against the rusty window screen, the curtains fluttering in the night. Not a song but a plea, the cry of a spirit.

Beat 2

Mama rolled biscuit dough on a dish towel covered with flour. The sun flowed in the window above the kitchen sink.

111

"Do you want to cut them out for me?" she asked and offered me the drinking glass.

I dusted it with flour and pressed out the biscuits in perfect rows, not wasting a bit of dough.

Mama placed each perfect round circle on a baking sheet. "I made extras so you could have snacks today."

"I thought you didn't go to work until three."

"I have to meet the supervisor and fill out paperwork. Don't worry. I grew up in this house. You'll be fine."

"I heard a voice last night. At first I thought it was singing."

"Maybe you dreamed it."

"I wasn't dreaming, Mama."

She raised an eyebrow. "What was this voice saying?"

"She was real sad and begging for someone to take her home."

"The hospital is just on the other side of the pecan grove. You probably heard a patient."

"She was so sad."

"A lot of people over there are really sad. Your granny looks after one lady who has a tea party every day at two. She has fancy porcelain china and insists that your granny drink tea with her." She shook her head. "Lots of people who go in there are normal as normal can be, but they don't stay that way for long. I don't want you on the hospital grounds."

A chill walked up my backbone.

Beat 3

Never tell a twelve-year-old not to do something. She will bust a gut doing it. As soon as Mama was gone, I went to the fence that separated Granny Esther's yard from the pecan grove. In the corner the fence was loose, and I pulled it up from the ground and pushed through on my stomach. The pecan grove was free of brush and a cool breeze wrapped me in a hug. A million sets of eyes—belonging to who or what, I didn't know—watched me as I walked through the trees into the clearing. A building with three floors and rows of windows sat in the middle of it.

"Little girl, what are you doing here?" A short old woman bent in the shoulders, wearing a crisp blue uniform, looked me over from her washtub, where she stirred something in the water with a long wooden paddle.

I shrugged.

"Hadn't your mama taught you any manners? Shrugging is a nasty habit." She waved her hand at the building. "They could think you belong in one of those rooms, you know. You shouldn't be here."

I backed up a few steps.

"I know each and every patient in this place. Lots of regular folks are here. Folks that don't belong. You don't want to end up like that, do you?"

I found my voice. "I heard a woman calling for help last night." Some of the windows were opened, white curtains moving in and out with the breeze.

"This place is a death sentence. Take yourself home." She turned her back to me.

"I just want to help."

"No child, you can't help a person here. Get home now."

I slid back into the protection of the trees and didn't look back until I squeezed under Granny Esther's fence.

"Hey." A voice came from behind me in the grove.

"Hey yourself."

A short scrawny white boy walked out. "Bet you're wondering who I am."

"Naw, not even giving you a second thought."

"You heard Lina yelling last night. Didn't you?"

"Maybe." I licked my dry lips.

"You living here now?" The boy looked like the wind could blow him away.

"That ain't your business."

"The lady who lives here is nice to my grandma. Takes her food now and then. She lives the next street over. Grandma won't eat the food because she's afraid your grandmother might poison her, 'cause she's colored and all."

"My granny wouldn't do that to anyone."

"I know. My grandma is crazy as a loon."

"Why didn't she go to that hospital?"

He laughed. "Her family is known in this town. Nobody's going to mess with her."

"My mama and granny work at the hospital."

"A lot of folks do." He gave me an odd look. "I know about Lina. She worked for my grandma. She used to sing to me when I was just a little thing. Sang real good." The boy held his head up straight. "Hear that? My grandma is calling."

"I didn't hear nothing."

"I did. I got to go before she gets in a dither. Meet me here at midnight. I'll show you just where Lina is. If you want to know."

"Well, maybe. But what's your name?"

"Jeffery." He slipped back into the trees and was gone.

Beat 4

Granny sliced a block of fatback for frying and stirred the pot of pinto beans that had been cooking most of the day. "You want to help me make some cornbread? I like mine with a little sugar."

"You like sugar a lot." I laughed.

"You done pegged me after one night." She turned the flame on under the tin coffee pot. "How was your first night?"

"Good enough." I shrugged and thought about the the voice.

"What happened in North Carolina that shook up your mama enough to leave?"

I shrugged.

Granny poured a small amount of coffee into her china teacup saucer and filled the cup up. "Well, something happened." She gave me a look that made me want to squirm. "That man wouldn't tolerate your mama leaving and coming here."

"Why you drinking your coffee out of your saucer?"

"It's perfect for cooling hot coffee. My mama taught me that. She came from Europe, where Daddy was a doctor before the war came and her family had to run. My mama was white and my daddy was black, Emmaline. Did you know that?"

"No ma'am."

"See, there's mysteries in every family. Like that mean old daddy of yours letting you two just walk off and catch a train."

I didn't breathe a word. The phone rang and made me nearly jump out of my skin.

Granny Esther scooted her chair back. "It's probably Widow Bailey down the road, needing a can of Burton.

Lord, she goes through that snuff. Nasty habit." She put the receiver to her ear. "Hello?" She waited a minute. "Hello? Who's there? I don't know who's playing tricks but you better stop." She hung up the phone.

We settled down in front of the TV together after eating dinner and doing the dishes. "It's time for my show. *The Lone Ranger*. You'll love it, Emmaline."

I wanted to tell her I'd love anything because I'd never got to watch a TV before.

The phone rang again just a little into the show about a cowboy who wore a mask.

"Who could that be?" Granny Esther got up from the sofa. "Watch it for me."

She was back in a minute. "Somebody is messing around with me. Making prank calls."

At eleven o'clock we watched the news. And right there on that dern TV was home. Just pretty as you please. We'd made the Georgia news. Seems the place where Mama would sing when Daddy went there drinking had burned to the ground. One black man had been found dead, but they had no name.

Mama came in the kitchen door singing a song she sang for Daddy all the time. "What you doing up, Emmaline? Get to bed. You're taking advantage of your granny."

"Oh now. The girl hasn't never seen a TV. We was having a good time watching my programs. It's summer."

Mama ruffled my hair. "To bed."

I left, hoping she wouldn't come in looking for a conversation. Midnight was almost here.

Third Measure
Beat 1

"Rachel, somebody called here twice and didn't say a word. That's never happened."

The alarm clock ticking next to my bed read 11:30.

"Who could it be?" Mama sounded like she was in the hall.

"You don't think it's John, do you?"

Mama was quiet a minute like she was thinking on something. "I'm pretty sure we won't hear nothing from John, Mama."

"Well, it sounds like something he'd do."

"Don't worry about him."

Mama cracked the door to my room. I kept my eyes closed and breathed steady. She closed it back. Why was she so sure Daddy wouldn't make the calls? Probably 'cause he didn't have a phone to use.

When I heard snores coming from the bedroom Granny and her shared, I put my feet on the floor. A ping on the window nearly made me jump out of my skin. Stupid Jeffery stood in the milky glow of the moon. I slid the screen out and dropped to the grass. That's when I seen her. A white figure coming toward the fence. I pushed up against the house and stupid Jeffery just stood there.

"Take me home. My name is Lina Hunter." The voice echoed through the air. "Lord, please take me home." The white figure hovered at the fence but I couldn't make out her face. Then finally she moved back to where she came from, disappearing into the trees.

"That was her." Jeffery stood looking at me. "She's trying to figure out how to get off the hospital property."

"Is she alive?" I didn't move.

"Yeah. Nothing about her is a ghost." He started walking to the fence. "Let's catch up with her."

"How you know so much about ghosts?"

"Ah, come on. I came here thinking you were brave."

"I am."

When I got to the fence, Jeffery had already squeezed through the hole and was holding the fence for me. The pecan grove was dark with shadows. When we got to the edge of the clearing, the moonlight shown on the lawn with a holy glow.

"Look, there she is." Jeffery pointed to the figure dancing on the lawn.

My heart seized in my chest.

"Take me home, take me home. Please." The figure twirled. "Let me out."

A light from the door of the building flashed onto the grass. "Lina, you don't want me to give you a shot tonight, do you?" Maybe this woman was a nurse. "If you don't stop that yelling and leaving the room, I will have no choice. Not on my shift. We discussed this." The woman wore a uniform and took the figure's hand. "If you do this again, I'm going to give you the needle."

The figure stopped dancing and hung her head. In the light of the door, she didn't look like a ghost, only a small black woman in a nightgown. "I won't do it anymore tonight." The door shut.

Jeffery and me ran back into the pecan grove.

"Tomorrow night I'm going back to get her out," I said.

"You're crazy. How?"

"I'll get her out of that room and show her the hole in the fence."

"She's a grown woman, too big to fit. And what's she going to do if she gets out? Where's she going? There ain't no family left. Anyway, you can't. You're just a girl."

I balled up my fist. "Take it back."

"You can't hurt me."

"You're too chicken to help."

"Naw. I'll be here."

Beat 2

The next morning before Granny Esther left for work, the phone rang. Again no one would speak to her.

"Do you think it's your daddy?"

"Who knows. He's liable to do anything. But he don't have no phone."

Granny Esther nodded. "It's probably some kids playing pranks."

The day went swimmingly and Granny Ester made fried chicken when she got home. I was starting to get used to her house. The phone rang right before bedtime.

Granny Esther's voice floated from the kitchen. "That was your mama. She has to work a double shift. If you need me, just call my name out."

Sneaking out to help Lina would be so much easier without Mama home.

❦

At midnight, I scooted out the window. In the distance, the sky lit up with a storm. Jeffery waited in the cover of the pecan trees.

"What's your plan?" His hands were jammed in his

pants pockets.

I held up a flashlight I'd found earlier in the kitchen drawer. "I'm going to signal her." I slid under the fence.

The windows were opened to the night air. The sky flashed with light, closer this time. I walked toward where I thought Lina's window was.

"Girlie, I told you to stay away." The old washerwoman stood in front of me, and she looked meaner at night.

My heart beat hard in my chest, but I stood my ground and looked her in the eyes. "I ain't leaving."

"You." The old woman pointed her finger at Jeffery. "This ain't your place to be. Git out of here."

"I don't believe in ghosts." I stepped in front of Jeffery.

The old woman laughed with the cackle of a witch. "You better believe. They be all around you." She blew away like dust on a windowsill.

I flashed the light on what I was sure to be Lina's curtains. "Lina," I whispered real loud.

The curtains stirred. "Who's there?"

"I'm here to help you."

"Are you messing with me?"

"No ma'am. Come down here and I'll show you how to get past the fence."

"Don't you leave. I'm coming."

The light in Lina's room spilled out on the lawn. "Lina Hunter," a voice said. "I warned you."

"Someone is here to help me."

"Girl, you can't go anywhere. You know that. Why don't you just give up?"

"But there's someone down there ready to help me. Just look."

I should have spoken up, but I stayed quiet and so did

Jeffery.

"You lay down. I'll get your medicine." The window shut hard. The nurse didn't even bother looking.

Two barred owls called back and forth.

"Let's get out of here. I told you she can't leave," Jeffery whispered.

"I can't just leave her."

"You're a fool if you think you can do anything else." Jeffery was moving to the tree line.

I followed. What else could I do? One little girl couldn't save no full-grown woman who was probably crazy. "Jeffery, we got to help her."

"Ain't nothing we can do. I'm tired. I got to get back to my grandma."

I pushed through the hole in the fence. "I can't just give up on her."

"She's stuck. A lot of folks get stuck." And Jeffery was gone.

I hightailed it to my window, and as I crawled in, I saw a shadowy figure sitting in the chair beside the bed. Thunder rumbled across the sky. My legs went boneless.

"You want to tell me what you're doing out of this house?" Granny Esther flicked on a lamp.

Silence.

"I reckon I can call your mama at work."

"I was trying to help someone."

"Who you helping after midnight?"

"It's a long story."

"You best be telling me."

"There's a woman, Lina Hunter, who calls from the hospital every night. She needs help."

"Lord, child. You can't help Lina."

"Jeffery said the same thing."

"Who is Jeffery? There's no Jeffery around here."

"He lives the road over at his grandma's house. Her name is Bailey. He said you take her food sometimes."

Granny Esther's breaths were long and deep. "This Jeffery is a liar. Nobody lives with Mrs. Bailey. She's alone. Mrs. Bailey is crazy and alone. Ain't no telling what will come out of her mouth. She's not all there." Granny Esther shook her head. "A long time ago she had a daughter and a grandson, but both are dead now. The daughter drove their car into a tree doing a hundred miles an hour. Made Mrs. Bailey go crazy. She told folks someone murdered them. Lina Hunter was her maid before she got put in the hospital for stealing the old woman's money."

"Lina stole money?"

"I doubt it. Folks like Lina and me—even you, Emmaline—can get in trouble for nothing. Sent away, killed even. It's just a fact. Happens all the time." She gave me a long, sad look. "We can't do a thing to help Lina. Go to sleep, child." Granny stood up.

"I'll tell Jeffery tomorrow what you said."

"Seems to me he might be a haint, child. Walking this earth because his business ain't finished. His mama killed them both. Now go to sleep."

As soon as she closed the door, the phone rang.

"You need to quit calling here." She slammed the phone down.

Beat 3

Granny left half an hour before Mama was due. I ate a biscuit and got dressed. There was a knock on the door. I opened it expecting to see Jeffery, expecting he couldn't be no spirit.

Daddy, clean and fresh, sober, stood before me. "I've come for you and your mama, Emmaline. It's time to come home."

"She ain't here."

"Well, are you going to invite me in?" He gave a short laugh and worked his way around me. "Smells good. I'll take one of those biscuits."

Beat 4

By the time Mama came through the door, Daddy was settled at Granny Esther's table with a couple of biscuits and some of her homemade blackberry jelly. "I do like me some jelly, Rachel."

Mama's eyes turned wild. "Emmaline, go to your room."

"No ma'am." I wasn't in the habit of talking back, but that look on her face told me she might do anything. I wasn't losing my mama to prison.

She turned her look on me.

"I'm staying right here with you, Mama."

Mama whipped her attention back on Daddy. "I'm not sure why or how you came down here looking for us, but you're not welcome. All I have to do is call the sheriff. This town knows Mama and me. You'll be in jail faster than you can stand up and leave the house."

"Now Rachel, you know darn well we're still married, and I'm the boss of this family." He didn't have a clue, even sober, when to be quiet.

Mama took a step toward him. "Family? Ha. We're not your family. Marriage has nothing to do with us, John. I'm divorcing you as soon as I have the money. Get on out. We don't want you around. Go back to North Carolina."

Daddy stood but made no effort to come toward Mama. "You don't tell me what to do, woman. I'll take you back if I see fit."

Mama took the cast-iron skillet from its hook by the stove. "Just try." She raised it.

Daddy stepped back, scrubbing the chair on the floor. "You've changed, Rachel."

Mama's laugh was mean. "It's about time I stopped putting up with the likes of you." She stepped around the table, holding the iron pan high. "Get out of town. Now. I would love to use this pan on you. The trouble you've caused in my life is worth every time this skillet lands on you. Go. Before I do it." She moved closer.

Daddy stumbled into a chair, pushed it down, and made for the door. "That's fine, gal. I came back here to give you a second chance. You just messed up with me."

Mama drew the pan back. "I said get."

Daddy was gone from the house as quick as he'd appeared.

Mama put the pan on the stove. "I hope you don't mind living here with your granny for a while until we can get our own place," she said to me.

Finally I found my words. "Not a bit, Mama."

"Good. We don't even have to worry your granny with this."

"Yes ma'am." But I knew nothing much would scare Granny Esther.

"I'm going to sleep before I go back to work this afternoon. You can lock the door if you want, but he won't be back."

"I ain't scared." And I was telling the truth.

When Granny Ester got home that afternoon, Mama was leaving out.

"Rachel, I heard there was a stranger looking around town for you."

Mama huffed. "This town still talks about everyone's business. I handled it just fine. Won't be no more problems."

"I raised you good." Granny Esther gave me a wicked smile and added, "Tomorrow I'm taking Emmaline to the hospital with me."

Mama frowned. "I don't want her working around there."

"Ain't about working. I got someone I want her to meet. She'll be perfectly fine."

"Okay." Mama looked at me. "Is that okay with you?"

"Sure." I couldn't tell them I was frightened to death of the place already. What was Granny up to?

Mama left the house humming a sweet tune.

That night was too quiet, not even a heat bug. I watched out the window a long time after Granny and Mama fell asleep. Once I was sure I saw a white shadow move through the pecan grove. I wanted to see if Jeffery would show up. Maybe I had imagined him.

∽

Granny packed me a peanut butter and jelly sandwich and an apple. "Through the summer I will need you every Thursday."

"What will I do?"

"You'll see." Granny Esther gave me a wink.

∽

125

The hospital loomed like a bad dream. My heart beat hard in my chest. Why had I agreed to go?

"Come on, Emmaline." Granny Esther stood outside of the car.

I took a deep breath and got out.

"You told me you wanted to help," she insisted.

Had I?

"I have someone for you to meet in a proper way." She led me around the corner of one of the buildings. There were park benches and tables. Nurses dressed in white walked among the others, all women. One lady with thick glasses worked on sewing. Another waved at us. "Hello, Esther. Don't forget about tea today."

Granny Esther smiled. "Mrs. Baker, I wouldn't miss it."

"Who do you have with you today?"

Granny Ester gave me a nod. "This is my granddaughter, Emmaline. She lives with me now."

"Well, you must bring her to tea."

"She will be busy today, but maybe another day." Granny Esther scooted me along with a gentle push.

We sat at an empty picnic table. Granny gestured toward a small woman walking with a nurse. In the daylight, dressed in blue pedal pushers and a white blouse, Lina Hunter looked like someone else, timid and scared.

The nurse saw Granny and led Lina toward us.

"Emmaline," Granny said, "this is Lina Hunter. I think you two have met." She turned to Lina. "My granddaughter, Emmaline, is new in town. She's heard you calling at night."

Lina took a seat at the table, looking at her hands. "I'm sorry, young lady, if I frightened you."

"You didn't, ma'am," I assured her.

Granny Esther leaned over the table. "I have two sack

lunches here for later. Would you entertain my girl while I work, Lina?"

Lina looked me in the eyes for the first time. "Yes, Miss Esther, I'll keep her company." She ran her fingers through her dark curly hair. "I've seen you before with Jeffery. He visits now and then. He's a good boy. Of course I've known him since he was a baby."

Granny Esther looked startled and raised her eyebrows, but she made no comment about this. "I'll leave you two talking," she said, winking at me again. "I'll be back to get you after tea."

That's how I got to know Lina Hunter. I visited her every Thursday that summer and on into the fall after school started. She told me stories about her childhood, and I told her my dream of becoming a nurse.

"Lord, Emmaline, think bigger than that," she pleaded. "Be a doctor. Us folks need a good doctor."

I visited Lina off and on all the way through high school up until I left for college in Atlanta. We promised to write, but somehow I knew Lina wouldn't. That didn't matter. We were still friends.

Fourth Measure

Mama sat in the third row from the front when I accepted my college diploma. She cheered at the top of her lungs and broke out singing "Amazing Grace." Everyone clapped. Afterwards she turned a bright smile on me and gave me a bear hug that reminded me of the one Granny Esther gave me the first time I met her.

"You're a sight for sore eyes, girl. Your granny is so proud. She's down in her knees again or she'd be here."

127

"I know she would. I'll see her before fall."

"You'd better before you go off to New York City. Medical school. My girl. Who would have thought we'd have a doctor in our family?" Mama's face grew serious. "Your granny wanted you to know that Lina Hunter slipped out of the hospital last week and no one has been able to find her. You remember her?"

Of course I remembered Lina Hunter. If not for her, I would never have thought of being a doctor. "Wonder where she went?"

"Your granny guessed she took out to Mississippi where her sister lives. She's still young enough to make something of her life."

"She always seemed a lot older to me."

"She surely loved you."

"I loved her too."

Mama gave me another hug, holding on tighter than before.

᪐

That summer I learned life wasn't exactly what I thought. The summer I saw my first ghost, Jeffery, and didn't even know he was a ghost until he was gone. The summer of Daddy's empty, silent calls. The summer Mama left Daddy—her strongest moment, her shining grace. If not for her courage, I wonder what would have become of us. I surely wouldn't have gone to medical school. I thought about Lina on her own, finding her way across the South. I could still hear her voice turning into a morning breeze, swirling in the trees and settling into the wind, her words tangled in the hot summer air. *Take me home.*

A TOUCH OF MOUNTAIN MAGIC

1969

Big red barn will forever mean childhood to me. Playing hide-and-seek in all the nooks and crannies while rain taps on the metal roof. Sleeping bags spread out in the hayloft on hot summer nights while we scared ourselves sleepless with ghost stories. —Paula Sannar Niziolek

My bicycle. Santa brought it for Christmas when I was six years old. Even though it was only a 24-inch, it was still too big for me until my Daddy took some wooden blocks and screwed them to the pedals, making them thicker so my legs would reach. Sixty-five years later, I still have the bike. —Teresa Martin Gregory

My blanket. I carried it everywhere. It had a certain comforting smell. I had another one just like it, and I couldn't be tricked into using the other one, though Mama tried. I was four.—Letitia Crawford

Sometimes the silence in my head turns me inside out. I'm the only kid in this big old house, with a mama that is two sheets to the wind most of the time. I don't mean she drinks. She doesn't have to drink. Sweet Jesus, she's just a little removed from the world the rest of us walk around in each day. She is the worst company, always muttering to herself, carrying on all kinds of conversations but not one with me. I can't figure out how Mama holds a job down at the natural gas company in Asheville, answering customer phone calls all day.

"One day I'm going to lose my mind and destroy every gas bill for fifty miles. Wonder what my bosses would do then? All the bigwigs sitting around sipping their mint juleps will have their asses in a sling." This is something she threatens often, so much so I worry I'll be watching the nightly news and there she'll be, going to jail handcuffed. *Woman destroys gas bills for all of Asheville.*

Each night just as the sun starts sinking into the treetops in front of our house on Black Mountain, Mama eases up the pitted and rutted drive. I, Abigail Owen, do what any good daughter should do. I put our supper of Oscar Meyer wieners and cold pork-n-beans from the can on the table. We eat the same thing for supper every night, with the exception of Fridays when Mama stops in Asheville to buy an eight-piece box of Kentucky Fried Chicken. She always stops at the 7/11 and buys six ten-ounce glass bottles of ice-cold Coke from the cooler. The sweat runs down my arm when I turn the bottle up. Fridays are the best. After Mama finishes her food, she changes into her blue or black or red neglige covered in lace. Underneath she doesn't wear a stitch of clothes. She flounces around the house, showing me everything she has like I don't even exist. Sometimes I think I don't. She never really sees me until she needs something.

Weekends, Mama watches old black-and-white movies. I hate the old ones like that. Give me some color any day. This is the one real rebellion I allow my twelve-year-old self. On special weekend nights, she crawls into her bed piled high with fluffy pillows and invites me to do the same. We watch something modern, fun, a sitcom. Mama barely leaves the bed until Monday, when she begins the routine all over again.

Sometimes I think I'll go completely out of my mind.

Stir crazy. There is only so long I can stare at the inside of a house. If I dare peek out her bedroom drapes at night, she yells.

"Shut that curtain. Abigail, don't you go standing in the open window. This place is dangerous. There's always some man out there waiting to look in, to see us alone in here. It's a dangerous place."

Lord, I would love to see some danger, something, anything. I am way too selfish feeling like this. We live in the cabin without any payments. Granny—Mama's mama—left the whole place to her only child when she died two years ago. On her deathbed she told me not to leave my mama behind, to always look out for her. Of course I promised. I was only ten years old. What was I supposed to do? Daddy saw Granny's death as the perfect opportunity to dump Mama. He dropped her and me on the doorstep of this house and took our only car.

"Bell, you look after Abigail. I'll be back soon enough." We both knew that was a lie.

Thank goodness Granny Owen left us her car. Part of me understands why Daddy left. Darn, I want to leave just like him. I hate him for leaving me behind. Many times I wish I had a sister, even a brother, so at least I would have some company besides my crazy mama. A sister would have been nice. No kids from school want to step foot on the property. Mama's craziness walks a mile in front of her.

But she isn't so bad. I only get one set of parents. Mama has a special gift of turning Christmas into the best time ever. Her favorite song is "Silver Bells" sang by Andy Williams. She blasts it from the portable record player beginning the day after Thanksgiving. And until Christmas arrives, she spends every single penny of her paycheck each week on presents. We even have a shiny aluminum foil tree with a color wheel that reflects the colors of the rainbow. But none of this makes up for her being so doggone weird.

The first time I saw the strange girl, much older than me, I was in the big red barn out back, up in the loft, where I go to think or get away from Mama. That barn is the absolute best thing about living on the mountain. I stretch out on my back in the hay, looking at the old dark beams and feeling real sorry for myself. Now, I don't like admitting to this, but I still have my baby blanket. I keep it close to me all the time, especially since Daddy left. Mama threatens to throw it away, tries to trick me by putting another one—exactly like it—in its place while she washes the filthy real thing. So the blanket is tucked up under my head, touching my scalp, giving me good thoughts about the time Daddy bought me a beautiful red bike when I was five and my feet wouldn't even touch the pedals. Mama swore I'd kill myself on it, but Daddy fixed it. He attached big blocks of wood on the pedals and the problem was solved. Daddy is like that, a problem-solver; just when you think there isn't no solving, he works a miracle .

The girl bends over me and looks me straight in the eyes.

"What you doing in my barn?" I want to sound good and mean since she's probably some of that danger Mama talks about all the time.

The girl watches me. Her long hair is a mixture of blonde and a touch of honey that makes the strands glow. Her nose and eyes seem familiar, as if I know her. "You look sad, little girl. You won't always be, you know."

"I ain't little. I'm twelve and I sure ain't sad." I push up to a sitting position.

"You won't always be lonely. Twelve is a hard time, especially if you don't have a dad." She twists at a thread of her hair and smiles.

"I have a dad, thank you. He's just not here right now. He doesn't like my mama anymore and left for awhile. She's crazy. But he loves me."

"My dad left when I was four." She folds her arms over her chest. "I feel like we know each other."

The girl looks real, not like some ghost story. If I touch her, she will be skin and bones. I am sure of it. "Do you remember your dad? It's been two years since I've seen mine. Sometimes I think I've forgotten his face."

"He writes me. But I don't really have a face for him. Sometimes just as I'm waking, I know exactly how he looks. He's there, tucked away in my thoughts. Do you like your dad?"

"That's a stupid question. I might be mad at him but I love him. Shoot, he's better looking than Paul from the Beatles."

"I think we should know each other." The girl studies my face.

"What's your name?" I ask.

"Emily. What's yours?"

"Abigail."

"That's a good name." Emily looks over the top of my head as if she sees someone, and then she is gone.

From this moment forward, if things get bad with Mama, I think of Emily. Never once do I think I am losing my mind like Mama. I guess the way Emily sounded like a real girl and is so much older than me puts me at ease. If I was going to make up a girl, she would be my own age.

Thinking about Emily always makes me feel happy.

Right before Halloween, one of the worst things that could happen does. Jane Carter, who rides the bus, sees my blanket sticking out of my backpack and grabs it. She is mean and hateful to any of the girls younger than her, a real bully.

"What is this thing?" She stands and opens the blanket covered with pink lambs, stained and dingy. "Is this your baby blanket?"

All the kids laugh on cue. No one crosses Jane Carter.

"Give it here." I reach to grab the cursed thing.

Mr. Carl, the bus driver, looks in the big mirror. "Jane, give that back, and you got two days of detention."

"You can't give me detention. You're just the bus driver," Jane sasses.

"I'll turn this bus around and take you back to the school." Mr. Carl glares at her.

She throws the blanket at me, and the look she's wearing tells me what will happen the next day.

As I walk to the front of the bus—thank goodness Jane doesn't live on Black Mountain—she sticks her big foot out and catches mine, causing me to fall face-first into the aisle. All the kids laugh, especially the ones getting off at my stop. I walk real slow so they can get ahead of me.

Cathy Hoffman, a year younger than me, stops. "Jane probably has her own blanket. Don't worry about what she says."

My cheeks heat. "But everyone is afraid of her so it doesn't matter."

Cathy shrugs. "I know." She turns into her driveway. "I don't think you're stupid."

"Thanks."

When I get to our drive, I check the mail. I never check the mail, but today I open the rusty mailbox door. Three envelopes. My fingers tingle. Granny would have said that's a sign of magic. As soon as I see the loopy handwriting on one of the envelopes, I know it's from Daddy. It is addressed to me. I stare at the paper in my hand for the longest time before I open it real slow like.

Abigail:

I'm sending you another letter. I hope you are getting these. I would rather you were mad at me than think your mom is keeping the letters from you. I can get why you're mad. I would be mad too if my dad left me high and dry. And this isn't all your mom's fault. It would be so much easier to blame it on her and her illness, but the truth is I've done this before. Anyway, I wanted to tell you a secret I've kept for a long time. You have a sister. Your mom didn't want you to know I was married before. I think it is time you know. I left her mom when she was four so she really doesn't know what I look like. I don't visit because her mother hates me for good reason. See, Abigail, I'm not a good husband or father. But please don't hate me too much. I wanted you to know about your sister so you can write to her. Below is her name and address. She is much older than you. I have let her know you will be writing and have given her your address too. Please get to know her.

Love,
Your Father
Your sister's address:
Emily Owen
2561 Denton St.
Marietta, GA 30060

I hold the letter a long time, staring at the red barn, my place to think. A sister. Could she be the Emily I met not so long ago? Not a ghost. But how had I seen her? Granny would say, "Just a touch of mountain magic, Abigail. Just a touch of mountain magic." I know my life will never be the same again. If I hurry, I can sneak to the red barn and write my sister a letter before Mama gets home. I have a sister, and this changes my life, my loneliness.

A sister. Emily.

DANCERS ON THE HORIZON

1967

I was about twelve when I got the old mystery date game.—Sherry Brooks

The gray snowy light seeped from the sky when the front door, which was never locked probably never had a lock, opened. In walked Mama looking prettier than she had ever looked. Snowflakes dotting her dark hair. Even a couple on her eyelashes. She turned and waved. A truck backed up and turned around.

"I'm starving, Grandma." Mama tossed her purse on the sofa.

"Didn't Mrs. Tucker feed you some of that fine fruitcake she makes every Christmas?"

Mama gave Grandma Connor a half smile. "She tried. That stuff is poison in the worst way."

Grandma nodded with what seemed like a giggle. "There are stories about folks dying only hours after one bite."

Mama full out laughed. "I hope we have fried chicken."

Grandma raised an eyebrow. "With that pretty little figure?"

Mama flipped a long curl away from her face. "It doesn't really matter up here."

"So David isn't worth pleasing?"

A look of surprise spread over Mama's smooth face. "He's my friend, Grandma. My buddy from childhood."

"I wonder what he would say if I ask him how he felt."

Grandma Connor turned to the kitchen. "Come, Mary. I'll teach you how to make fried chicken. Your mother can set the table and make us a green salad."

Mama followed us, giving me a little love pinch on the arm.

Grandma Connor had been around forever. She wasn't even my real grandmother, more like my great-grandmother. She was my Pawpaw Oshie's mama. He grew up on Black Mountain, and when Mama finally left Daddy for good, Pawpaw decided the best place for us was right here at his childhood home. Daddy could be right dangerous when he was mad at Mama. We had been with Grandma for less than a week. I was adjusting but I missed my friends at home. But it felt like a second home for Mama, since she'd spent every summer with Grandma Connor until she got too big for her britches. At least that's how Grandma told the story.

⤚

The crust on the fried chicken was just the right crisp and had to be the best chicken I'd ever eaten in my life. The three of us sat around the small round table in the large farm kitchen.

"All my boys used to sit here every evening for supper." Grandma Connor spooned out a helping of green beans on my plate.

I looked at Mama because she knew I hated vegetables and never made me eat a one. She tilted her head to the side as if to say, eat them and be quiet.

So I did. Nothing had ever tasted so good, salty and sharp. If Grandma Connor could make hated vegetables taste that good, she was a magician or a witch.

"Grandma," Mama started as she helped herself to the salad laced with carrots and tomatoes.

"Yes, Rebecca."

"Mary saw the dancing haint on our way up the mountain Monday." She wrinkled her nose.

I had seen a woman that stepped out of the woods and stared at Pawpaw Oshie's car as we passed by. Her blonde hair framed her face, and her clothes were old, like from a long time before. Pawpaw Oshie was back in Atlanta, or I'd ask him if he believed in ghosts.

Grandma Connor stopped buttering her cornbread. The snow had stopped falling and the scene outside the window was creepy and beautiful at the same time.

"You don't say? No one has seen her in a long time. That's because folks don't believe in such things anymore. They believe only what they can see and smell and taste. So half of them are walking around talking and carrying on with spirits and they be stupid and don't even know."

The hairs on my arm stood straight up.

"Folks nowadays know too much. They go to big schools that tell them ghosts don't exist and that the old folks made stories up to keep everyone in line. Silly foolishness."

At that moment, as the last tiny bit of gray light dimmed, a redbird perched on a snowy branch, shaking the snow away into a shower of dust.

"A redbird is looking in." The bird tilted his head back and forth as if he were trying to figure out who I was.

Grandma Connor started buttering her cornbread again. "That's the dead coming to visit us."

"What do you mean? It's a redbird. It's going to freeze to death."

"Redbirds can handle cold weather. That's why they stay

139

and winter over in the mountains. Eat your food," she directed me.

"What spirit is that redbird?" I said around a large bit of sweet cornbread.

Grandma watched the bird.

"It's Uncle Maynard, of course," Mama said. "He always showed up at suppertime when I was a kid." She laughed and sounded much younger. Her fancy heels were watermarked.

"You're probably right, Rebecca. You need to eat two more pieces of fried chicken. You're far too skinny." Grandma pointed her fork at Mama.

Instead of refusing like I thought she would, Mama chose a large crunchy breast from the platter and set it on her plate. "Yes ma'am. Tell Mary the story of the dancing haint, Grandma."

"I don't think she can handle it. She'll be too scared, Rebecca. You should be ashamed of trying to scare your own gal."

Mama gave me an innocent look.

"I don't scare too easy. I'm used to doing all kinds of things by myself."

Grandma Connor gave a little shake. "That probably scares me more than my story will scare you." And she gave Mama a frown. "I think it was back in 1924, might have been '25. There were two sisters, Inas and Bertha Hawkins, who lived on the next farm over. There was two years difference between the girls, Inas being the youngest at twelve and Bertha fourteen."

"She just happens to be twelve like me?" I asked.

"Yes ma'am, she was. You know twelve-year-olds are like a clean glass. You can see right through them, what they be thinking, what scares them, what they care about or don't care about for that matter. Inas and Bertha's daddy was a mean, mean man. He wasn't as mean as Hobbs Pritchard that lived on up the mountain a bit. I guess *he* was probably the meanest man on this mountain, but their daddy gave Hobbs a run for his money. Beat those girls just for plain fun. See, he didn't like it they were born girls and then their mama went and died. That was some questionable business but a story for another day. No, he wasn't happy with those two beautiful daughters. He worked them like boys." Grandma Connor stopped and looked out the now dark window. "No, he worked them like dogs from daylight to dusk. I was a young wife then and took it upon myself to bring them girls a cherry pie—I'm known for my pies—when I heard the older one, Bertha, was sick. The man met me on the porch and told me to take my business somewhere else. Had a shotgun in his hands. I didn't give him any lip, just left. I always felt guilty for that. I should have done something."

"Done what? He might of shot you." I wasn't even eating, I was so wrapped up in the telling.

"She should have gone around the back of the house and knocked on the girls' window," Mama chimed in, an urgent catch in her words. "They stayed in the coldest part of the house, probably why Bertha got sick."

"Naw, wasn't no cold from that shell of a house that made Bertha sick. Don't know what it was. But what I do know was them girls loved to dance. They danced at night in the fields outside our farm. Their daddy would have killed them if he caught them. They slid out the window on nights when a decent moon hung in the sky. They could be seen dancing together, holding hands. And sometimes one of my boys, small then, would see a third girl with them." Grandma

141

gave me a hard look. "That's how things go with haints. They look so real folks believe they are. Them girls would dance and dance, tumbling to the ground and climbing back to their feet. Didn't even need a stitch of music. Something only they could hear drove them to glide like one of them ice skaters gliding around a frozen lake."

"You ever seen a frozen lake, Grandma?" Mama asked.

"I don't see that it matters one iota, Rebecca." She turned to look back at me. "For a good month, them girls didn't show themselves. I kept asking James—that was your great-grandfather—if he'd heard anything about them. But he hadn't heard a word. Then one sunny, warm day in March, I looked up from turning my kitchen garden for planting and seen the oldest, Bertha, dancing across the field right toward me. I put my hoe against the fence and went to meet her. She came real close before she spoke. "Inas is very sad. That cherry pie you wanted to give me would be real nice for her." Grandma Connor stopped talking and took three big bites of green beans. "We can't let our food get cold." She pointed at my plate.

I took two bites of a crisp drumstick.

"Good. I told that child I'd have to bake one, and she said that was fine. I was still a young woman and didn't know as much about the Specter of Death like I do now."

"How you know about death?" Even I could hear the fear creeping into my voice.

"Well, child, I'm the oldest thing on this mountain be-sides the trees and such. All my friends have died off. One day and probably not long away, I'll die. Everyone will say oh, she had a really long life, and throw me in the cemetery up there close to the church."

"Don't say that. Mama and me have to have a place to

stay."

Mama's smile disappeared. "It's ok, Mary. Grandma will be around for a long time."

"You can't coddle the child, Rebecca. People die. It's part of our lives. Anyway, back to the cherry pie, and eat your food, Mary." She scooted a bowl of mashed potatoes toward me.

"What happened when you took the pie to the girls?" I asked, recovering from the horrible thought of Grandma Connor dying sometime soon.

"I walked up on that porch but very carefully. I was still thinking on that shotgun in Mr. Hawkins's hands. After I knocked on the door, I stepped back to the edge of the porch so I could make my getaway if needed. The old wooden door creaked open, and there stood the younger girl, Inas. Her eyes were red. She looked at the cherry pie and gave a weak smile. 'My sister would have loved that pie,' she said. I told her, 'She's the one who came and told me to bring you one because you were sad.' That girl's mouth fell open. 'You ain't lying to me, are you ma'am?' 'No, I never would,' I said. Really, I was getting pretty bothered with the whole thing. 'Just ask your sister.' The young girl dropped her head. Said, 'I guess you didn't hear.' 'Hear what?' 'Hear that Bertha died yesterday. My sister is dead.'"

Grandma Connor looked at me.

"So she was dead when she came here to tell you about the pie?"

"Yes, she was. But I couldn't tell. And the other mystery was the third person who danced with them girls. Inas told me it was their mother, and like I said before, she had been dead a good spell. Haints are real, and they walk around this world with us, girl. Don't forget that."

"I won't. How do you know I saw the dancing haint?"

Mama grabbed another piece of fried chicken. "Because she always met me in the same curve each summer as I arrived. I didn't see her this time because I'm too old."

"Fiddle-daddle," Grandma Connor fussed. "Hasn't got a thing to do with age. It has to do with if you're a seer. Your mama isn't anymore. It happens to a lot of grownups. What did this girl you saw look like?"

"She had blonde curly hair that framed around her face. Her dress was pretty but from an older time. She had green eyes. Very green."

Grandma slapped the table and made me jump. "Who wants cherry pie?"

I half expected the dancing haint to pop up and say she did.

∽

The next morning Mama came to the door of my room upstairs. "Are you awake, Mary?"

The light was weak, and something in my gut said she was up to no good. "Yes."

She pushed the door open. Her best dress hung perfect from the waist, and new, better shoes replaced the ones she'd ruined the day before. "I'm leaving for Asheville. I want to get some Christmas shopping done. We deserve a little fun."

I sat up. "How are you going?" I thought about the money tucked in the sock in my bag. A fifty-dollar bill Pawpaw Oshie slid over to me before he left for Atlanta. "I want to go."

"You can't, sweet pea. How could I surprise you? And besides, I don't have much money. Your grandfather didn't give me but a twenty. That will barely buy each of us a small gift." She stuck out her lip. Mama must have seen him give me the money. She knew. Maybe it was the fact that she just knew Pawpaw Oshie's tricks intended to make her behave. "But if you have some money, I'll take it and buy you some extra things. What was it you wanted?"

"A Mystery Date game." Before she could ask again, I dug in my sock and pulled out the money. "Here."

Mama's eyes lit up. "This will be the best Christmas ever. What do you want to get for Grandma?"

"Buy her a new dress, a pink one." I played along. We both knew she wasn't coming back. She would ditch me and find Daddy. The both of them would use the money up before anyone heard from them.

"See you this evening. Tomorrow is Christmas Eve, little girl. We're going to have a good one." Mama gave me a quick hug. "Tell Grandma I'll be home before dark."

But I knew she wouldn't. The same truck from the day before was waiting for her outside, and she got in. This guy was really stupid if he thought she was going off with him. She was just using him to get back to her lifestyle with Daddy, even if it meant the loan sharks getting her.

The truck rattled out of the snow-covered drive.

"She's gone again?" Grandma Connor stood in my door. "Yes."

She nodded. "Breakfast? I have pancakes. Lots of real butter. Lots of syrup."

A smile formed on my lips. "I'll be there after I get dressed. Mama said she'd be back by dinner."

Grandma turned to leave. "I'm sure she'll make the effort."

⤝

Grandma's pancakes were the best breakfast in the world. I smothered mine in butter with only a small amount of syrup. I was a strange child who preferred salty to sugar.

"So what do you want for Christmas besides some silly store-bought toy?" Grandma Connor sat down at the table with hot coffee.

"I really don't play with toys much." I confessed.

"What do you like then?"

"I love to read. Books can take you anywhere. When I'm grown, I will travel to places like London or Germany."

Grandma smiled. "Books are good. I like to read. The bookmobile comes up here every two weeks in good weather. I always get me an armload of books."

"What is a bookmobile?"

"Lord, child, you don't know? It's a library on wheels. A big bus full of books."

"That sounds fun."

"Yes. Maybe you will still be here when it comes back."

"Yes, maybe." The snow dripped off the eaves of the house as the sun slid in and out of the clouds.

"Looks like the snow may be gone before Santa gets here tomorrow night."

"Maybe." I didn't want to tell her there was no such thing, that I found out when I was little when Mama forgot to put out the toys until the next morning.

"I'm sure he will show up, even though I haven't seen nor heard from him since my youngest left home in 1949. Santa doesn't forget things like that. You know, coming to a house."

"Yes ma'am."

"So what you got in your head to do today?" Grandma Connor watched me from the other side of the table.

"I don't know. I wanted to go with Mama but she wouldn't let me."

"Well, she can't buy you gifts with you there." She stood. "I tell you what. Why don't you go take a walk, get to know this place? Ain't a soul going to bother you. Get some sweet air in them lungs. I got some things to do here. Dress warm. There's boots by the door if you want to try them."

≈

The big boots left oversized footprints across the field. I had no idea where to go, so I walked to the woods. The drips fell around like rain, but some snow still clung to the trees. A redbird flitted in and out of the trees ahead.

"Redbirds are the prettiest."

I gave a jump. A girl with mousy brown hair stood close by. She wore an overcoat too large for her. The hem was only a few inches from the ground.

"They are pretty. Where did you come from?" This was not the blonde girl I saw coming up the mountain, so I figured she must live around here.

"I live up the mountain just a tad. I'm out trying to find some good pinecones for Christmas gifts. We ain't got much money. Daddy is real tight with any he gets. And he don't cotton to celebrations like Christmas or birthdays. But I want some presents under the tree."

"How can pinecones be presents?" I thought of how my friends back in Atlanta would be counting the presents under the tree for them, countless gifts with different-colored foil paper.

"I got me some ribbons and buttons I've collected throughout the year," the girl said. "I will glue them on and use some glitter I bought with a dollar I found. They'll be right pretty when I finish, add some happiness to the day." She bent to examine a rather long pinecone. "It's just hateful that it snowed. They will have to dry by the fire before I can decorate them. I'll be pushing for time." She stood and looked at me. "You want to help?"

"I guess." What else did I have to do?

"Good. Look for the big long ones." She walked into the woods and I followed. "Where do you come from?"

"I'm here staying with my Grandma Connor for Christmas, anyway."

The girl looked at me. "She's the lady that makes cherry pies."

"Yes."

"They're good. She is really old."

"She's my great-grandmother."

The girl nodded. "Let's get these pinecones collected. I ain't got all day."

We wandered the woods for what seemed like at least an hour. Big chunks of snow began falling from the tops of the trees.

"Watch out," giggled the girl. "They are like giant snowballs."

I laughed.

She looked in her cloth bag. "I got a lot, probably too many. You want some?"

"Sure."

"I bet your granny's got some good stuff to decorate with." She handed me several pinecones, and I placed them in the pockets of the coat I'd borrowed from Grandma Connor.

The girl looked at the sky. "I got to get home. Daddy will be looking for his dinner. You can find your way back, right?" She was just going to leave me there.

"I guess. What's your name? I'm Mary."

"Just follow the path. It will take you right back to your field. You can't get lost. Wow." The girl pointed.

On the snow was a perfect red feather.

"A girl never finds a redbird feather." She picked it up. "This has got to be pure lucky."

"It's pretty," I offered.

The girl smiled. "Merry Christmas." And she handed it to me.

"Oh no, you found it."

"It don't matter none. I like giving gifts." She began to walk away.

"What's your name?" I called.

"Yours is Mary?"

"Yes."

The girl was disappearing into the thick trees. "Don't worry about your mama. She'll be back. I promise."

"What you do you mean? I didn't say I was worried about my mother." But the girl was gone. "Hey? Are you still there?" I twirled the feather around with my fingers. "I know you can still hear me. You're being hateful." But the air was only disturbed by drips of water. I made my way back to the field without any problems.

⋙

"I cooked us some vegetable soup and cornbread. I figured

HAINTS ON BLACK MOUNTAIN

we could eat it for lunch and then have some of that leftover chicken tonight. I ain't never been good at making a small amount of food."

I pulled the pinecones from the coat pockets and placed the redbird feather next to them.

"Oh my, look at your treasures, Mary. A redbird feather is indeed a beautiful find." She picked it up to have a better look. "You went into the woods to explore?"

"Yes, and I met a girl. She never told me her name, but she was looking for pinecones to make Christmas gifts. She actually found the feather and gave it to me."

"I can't imagine who it was. Most of the kids either live at the top of the mountain or the bottom. Not many left here since there's no school."

"She told me she lived up the mountain, and her daddy doesn't like Christmas. She wanted to make gifts anyway. She sounded pretty poor."

Grandma Connor watched me. "Poor is as poor does, Mary. I got me a feeling you been playing with a spook."

A cold shiver washed over me. "She was real."

"Yep. They seem that way sometimes. I'd be betting you was playing with Inas, one of the sisters we was talking about last night."

"No, this was a real girl." I needed her to be a real girl.

Grandma shrugged. "You're probably right. Most haints try to tell you something about your future or past."

I thought of how the girl told me not to worry about Mama, but I didn't open my mouth. I had no time for ghosts. That scared me a bit too much.

"Let's eat some soup. Then we'll go find us a tree. Lord, Mary, I can't remember the last time I had a tree in this house. You are good for me. We'll use those pinecones to help decorate it. And I know I have some decorations in the attic."

༄

"See that tree there." Grandma Connor pointed to a beauti-fully shaped tree in the woods where we were walking.

"That's perfect." I didn't want to confess to her that Christmas trees never happened at my house. Mama and Daddy were always too busy for such things as decorating. I did get gifts because they always felt guilty for leaving me alone on Christmas Eve to go to parties and gamble. Never coming home at a decent hour. Most of the time I felt like I was their afterthought.

Grandma produced a saw. "We got to cut it down. I ain't as strong as I used to be, Mary. You'll have to help me."

"I haven't ever used a saw."

"Well, it's about time you learned." She handed me the saw. I crawled under the low-hanging branches and posi-tioned the blade on the trunk. I pushed and pulled. Little bits of wood and bark flew. A white line of raw wood was revealed. The sweet smell of pine filled the air.

"How are you doing?" Grandma asked.

"It's going slow, but I'm not giving up."

For the next thirty minutes or longer I sawed. The cut grew deeper and deeper.

"Let's try pushing on it," Grandma Connor suggested. She pushed on the trunk with her boot, producing a loud pop. The tree fell backwards but was still attached to the stump by a section of wood. "Cut through that strip, and we're home free."

I sawed and sawed. My arms burned and sweat trickled

down my back. The strip of wood and bark gave and the tree was free.

"You did it," Grandma yelled, as happy as me. The day had turned darker with more clouds and was leaking away from us.

"Mama will love this," I said without thinking.

"Yes, she will." Grandma Connor grabbed the trunk of the tree and began pulling.

"Let me pull."

"You did all the cutting. I can pull." And pull she did, without a minute's problem. This made me think she could have cut through the tree with no problem too.

There was no sign of Mama when we got back to the house.

"We'll lean her near the door and look for the tree stand before dark gets here." The tree stood against the back door. "I think the old stand is in the barn. Then we'll take a lamp up to the attic for the decorations."

Dusk had settled around the farm when we came out of the barn with the old metal Christmas tree stand. "I love the color of the winter sky right before it turns night." Grandma Connor stood in the yard looking. "See. There's the Christmas star."

One star shown brighter than any other. "Daddy said he didn't believe there ever was a Christmas star."

Grandma clicked her tongue. "Well, he doesn't have a lick of sense, Mary."

This made me giggle. "You're right about that. He's in trouble all the time."

"See." She kept looking. "Your name is the same name of baby Jesus's mother. Mary. What a solid, soft name."

I had never seen myself as soft or solid. "Thank you."

"It's a good name. Happens to be mine too."

Thinking of Grandma Connor with a real name was confusing. "I've never thought of you having a real name."

She laughed. "Let's go find some decorations. Maybe your mama will be home by then for supper." She walked to the back door.

"Grandma Connor."

"Yes, Mary."

"I doubt Mama will come back any time soon. She took my fifty dollars that Pawpaw Oshie gave me. She's long gone. She never wanted to come back here anyway. Pawpaw made her to protect us from the loan sharks and Daddy's mess. She won't be home until the money is gone."

Grandma Connor was silent.

Somewhere there was an owl calling, and another answered.

"Well, we just don't know what's going to happen, Mary. We can say a prayer that your mama understands how important it is to be with family for Christmas. But we won't let her decision decide whether we are going to be happy or not. Come on inside." The screen door squeaked as she opened it.

Right before I turned away from the field still dotted here and there with snow, I saw a gauzy figure move out of the woods.

"What is that?"

"What?"

But the field was empty and dark now. And there was no way I ever saw anything. "Nothing. I thought I saw something."

"Too dark tonight. The dancers only come when the moon is out. Who knows, maybe the clouds will clear."

153

"Do you still see the dancers?" I asked.

"Of course, especially around Christmas."

❧

The attic was a real room with a window at each end and a wooden floor.

"The younger boys slept up here when they were all home. I would hear them cutting up and laughing at night, especially on Christmas Eve when they were supposed to be asleep."

"Pawpaw Oshie?"

"Yes. Until Maynard left and he got the room you're sleeping in. That was the room your mama stayed in when she came to visit in the summers."

"Did she ever come up here?" Mama as a little girl was hard to picture.

"I think maybe once or twice. She liked to dress up in the old clothes packed away. She'd put on my old church hats and march around the farm like she was Mrs. Astor herself." Grandma Connor turned up the gas lamp. A soft yellow light spread, showing many boxes and trunks. "Let's start over there. That's the older stuff. Maybe that green trunk."

I pulled the trunk to the center of the room and sat down in front of it. "This room is great. I would love staying up here."

"Well, if you don't leave too quick, we can fix you a place here. Mary, you can stay as long as you want or need."

Big fat baby tears filled my eyes, but thank goodness the light was so bad she couldn't see. I pushed open the lid. A

moldy smell filled the air. Soft brown paper, crinkled newspaper, sat on top of what looked to be a lot of ornaments.
"Look here."

Grandma pulled an old chair across the room and sat
down. "We have a lot to go through. Let's just choose the
best. The ones we can clean up and use. Maybe there will be
a few you'd like to keep. Here's one." She held a wooden
frog. "Your Pawpaw made this in grade school. Look how
good he carved the body."

The frog was dark brown with age, but all the markings
were there to make him look real. "He'll make a fine orna-
ment."

"Look at this. My mother made these for me when I
married. I turned them into angels when the first two boys
were born to represent them on the tree." She held what had
once been handkerchiefs but were folded to make angels
with wings. Pearls were sewn on the heads to make halos.

"Those are beautiful."

"They're yellowed, but lots of love and work went into
them." She looked at the trunk. "We need to eat. Let's take
these and come back for more after supper. Tomorrow we
will decorate the tree." She stood and glanced toward one of
the windows. "The moon is out, Mary. Watch for our haints
tonight."

⁓

Grandma Connor warmed our chicken in the oven and made
fresh biscuits to go with it.

"I don't think Mama's coming back." I stood at the front
room's window.

"Well, if David has anything to do with it, she'll be here.

He's a good man, believes in family. I'm guessing he picked her up this morning. Ain't no one else going to take her down the mountain but him."

"Mama pretty much does what she wants."

"I guess I know her as well as you. Remember, she used to spend her summers with me."

∽

After we brought the tree inside and got it to stand up straight, I went to bed.

"Don't worry about your mama. She'll be back. Christmas Eve is tomorrow." Grandma Connor said this from the doorway.

"She hasn't ever given two hoots about being around me at Christmas. There's a lot I could tell you."

Grandma stood there quiet.

"Both her and Daddy missed almost every Christmas Eve and some Christmas Days." A freedom was released in those words. Someone knew. I didn't have to hide how my parents didn't care about me. "You mentioned Santa. I've known since I was little there was no such thing. Mama and Daddy always forgot to put the presents out if they were home."

Grandma sucked in a breath. "Does your Pawpaw know about all this?"

I shook my head. "No. Wasn't no sense making more problems for Mama. She makes enough on her own. I take care of myself."

"Well, a girl your age shouldn't have to look out for herself. You should be a girl." Those words were laced with anger. And I was proud that she cared. "Get in that bed, and

I'll bring you a hot water bottle."

"What is that for?"

"I used to bring one to the boys when it was cold. Put it down at your feet."

"Ok."

The moonlight sprinkled across the bed. I listened to the house sounds and strained to hear footsteps on the front porch. The sound of the truck. Nothing. Not one part of me wanted to sleep. I needed a book. *Little Women* was in my suitcase, but I didn't want to wake Grandma Connor turning on the light. I slid out of bed, thinking I would close the door to my room so I could turn on the bedside lamp.

That's when I saw them. Two figures dancing in the field. Girls in long dresses or nightgowns. I stood at the window and watched as their bodies moved like they were listening to music. But the night was silent except for the owls still calling back and forth. Without thinking, I went down the stairs to the back door, expecting the girls to be gone. But they danced on in the snow, leaping and twisting. One was the blonde with curls. The other had dark hair. I opened the door and stepped on the porch. No music. Just cold floorboards, sending icy fingers up my legs.

The girls swayed and leapt into the air. What a treat to watch. They looked real enough to me. Not ghosts. Nothing was scary about them other than they danced in a field on December 23rd barefooted, with snow still on the ground.

I walked down two steps. Still the girls danced, moving together perfectly. "Who are you?" I called.

Both stopped and looked at me. They were too far away for me to see their faces well, but they watched me, saw me. "We are sisters."

"Why do you dance?"

"Why not? We dance because we loved to when we were alive."

The girls' mouths never moved. I just heard their answers in my head.

"Are you real?"

"Are you?" they answered back.

"Did you both die young?"

"Yes silly, that's why we come here to dance."

Then the dark-haired one turned to stare at me. "You shouldn't give up on your mama, you know. She's trying to come home. She's stuck."

"What do you mean?"

But they were gone. The moon shown on an empty field.

I ran back in the house. "Grandma Connor," I yelled. Her bedroom was on the first floor down the hall from the kitchen.

"What is it, child?" she called back as she came out of her room.

"I saw the ghost girls dancing."

"Did you now? I thought you were sleeping."

"I couldn't. I went outside. They talked to me. The dark-haired one said Mama is stuck. She's trying to come home but she's stuck. I think she needs help."

Grandma watched me for a long minute. "The haint said this to you?"

"Yes. How can we find Mama?"

She looked around the kitchen as if she might see an answer. "I don't know. We don't have a clue where to look. We have no way to go. Maybe we just have to wait."

"How can we just wait?" Tears were running down my face. I looked out the front room window. "If she's stuck, she needs me."

Grandma Connor touched my shoulder. "If we don't hear from her tomorrow morning, we'll walk to David Tucker's house. Find out if he came home. Right now we wait. That's all we can do until daybreak."

I knew she was right.

❧

I was awake as the first streak of gray light pushed through the window. The field was empty. Maybe I had imagined the whole thing, dreamed it.

"Are you up, Mary?"

"Yes ma'am," I called.

"Get down here and eat. If we're walking to the Tucker place, you'll need food. It's a good four miles up the mountain. Dress warm."

I obeyed, pulling on a thick sweater and wool pants.

Grandma Connor gave me hot biscuits and jelly while she drank her coffee. I took a good hard look at her, all the lines streaking down her face. "I'll walk up there, and you wait here in case Mama shows up."

"Don't mess with me, Mary. I know what you're up to, can see straight through you. I can walk farther than you any day. Don't count me old yet." She pulled on her big coat that looked like a man's, probably was. "Let's go. We're taking the woods. It's shorter and faster. All we got to do is follow the river."

I followed her to the west, where we entered the woods. There were still patches of snow here and there. The sound of the river grew louder as we moved up a narrow path. The breeze blowing off the water chilled me to the bone, even with the heavy coat and sweater. Mist hung over the river in places, resembling a ghostly image. The path turned steep and the rocks were coated with a layer of ice.

"Be careful, Grandma Connor. That's ice."

"I see it. You be watching out too. Neither of us need a broken hip." She picked her way up the rocks, testing the footing, grabbing small sapling trees.

A white figure moved across the path in the distance. "Someone is up there."

Grandma watched the path in front of her. "I don't see anything, but your young eyes are better than mine. Some old haint. These woods are haunted. Everyone knows that. Most old folks won't even walk through them."

"Why are we here?" A cold chill worked through my bones, and it had nothing to do with the temperature.

"So we can get to David Tucker's faster." She trudged on with me right behind.

Neither of us spoke for the longest time. I kept thinking of Mama. Where was she stuck? What would we find when we got to this farm? At least we were doing something. That's when I saw a roof.

"David Tucker's barn. We'll be there in no time." Grandma kept moving forward.

Mama could be there waiting, but I knew this was just pie-in-the-sky wishing.

A dog began to bark. In the pocket of the coat was the redbird feather. Luck. The barking got louder. Then out of nowhere a blur of a body dove past me and hit Grandma Connor with all its force. She went down hard.

The dog was growling over her.

I picked up a big stick and swung it in the dog's direction. "Go away. Go away."

Grandma had a dazed look on her face.

"Help us," I called out. "Help us."

A girl stood near the dog. She held out her hand and stared at him. The dog grew quiet and hung his head. "They are coming to help. Don't worry."

Grandma turned her head and looked at the girl. "Inas, is that you?"

The dark-haired girl smiled. "Yes ma'am. I stay in these woods a lot."

"I need to get up but my ankle is hurt."

"They're on their way, Mrs. Connor. Don't worry."

"You said my mama was stuck." I found my voice and spoke to the spirit.

"She is stuck and needs help. Stuck in her thinking, in her decisions."

"What does that mean? She isn't hurt?"

Inas gave me a pitying look. "The worst kind of stuck is in your head. She can't go in the right direction for spinning in circles. What seems right to me or you is confusing to her. Give her a chance, and don't judge." Inas looked behind her. "They're here." And she was gone.

A tall man with sandy-looking hair came through the woods. "Oh, Mrs. Connor, you're hurt." He looked at his dog, who still hung his head in shame. "Teddy, did you do this?"

"He didn't know any better." Grandma gave the dog, Teddy, a look of sympathy. "He was protecting his land. We cut through the woods to come see if you know where Rebecca is."

A rustle in the trees drew our attention. "What is going on?" There stood Mama in her fancy shoes, dressed to the nines in a new outfit. At least she was ok. But anger sprang to life in my chest in a way I'd never felt before. I tried to remember what Inas said about judging. "Where have you been? Grandma Connor is hurt because of you. She brought me here because we thought you were hurt somewhere. You only ever think about yourself, and you will never change." I stood close to Grandma. "She's old and walked through these woods to help find you. And here you are with new clothes, probably all the money gone. You are selfish." I spat the words at her.

"It wasn't like that," Mama said. "Not this time. I was stuck in Asheville. David came looking for me. It was late. I didn't want to wake you."

No one said anything for a minute. Then Grandma Connor spoke. "It's time to go home."

"You need a doctor," I insisted.

"Yes, I think you might be right, girl. I don't think anything's broken, but at my age, I can't be too careful." She looked at the man while Mama stood there with her mouth hanging open. "David, could you take me down the mountain? I miss the days when Maude Tuggle took care of us up here."

David smiled. "Yes ma'am. I'm going to pick you up."

"Be careful," I fussed.

"I will. You come ride with us. I may need your help." He turned a half smile on Mama. "Rebecca, you'll have to wait here at my house with Mama. We'll be back as soon as we can."

Mama didn't say a word. She petted the dog's head and walked him back to the house while David put Grandma Connor on the front seat of his truck.

✀

So my Christmas Eve on Black Mountain was spent in Asheville at the emergency room. It turned out that Grandma Connor had only sprained her ankle, but because of her age she was ordered to stay off of it for several weeks. We pulled into the yard just at dark. The moon was balanced on the trees. A crisp, cold air filled my lungs and reminded me how lucky I was to be there at that house. Lights shined on the inside, and we were hit with a blast of warm air as we entered, Grandma between David and me because she refused to be carried. Mama appeared, wearing what looked like a pair of men's pants and sensible flat shoes.

"Your mama loaned me some clothes to walk home in." Her cheeks turned pink as she spoke to David.

Under the tree were several brightly wrapped presents.

"I heated the soup, Grandma." This was a huge accomplishment for Mama.

I went to put the water on the stove for tea and glanced out the back window. The field was empty, but something told me the sisters would be back that night. They would dance in honor of Christmas. Me, I had so much to learn. People were never simple. Under the tree were gifts, and one of them would be that stupid Mystery Date game. The girl who wanted it was long gone, and Mama wouldn't understand this. She wasn't a seer. Not really. Some people stay exactly who they are their whole lives, while others move in and out of life, dancers on the horizon.

APPALOOSA WIND

1968

My grandmother picked green beans for Stockley's canning company. She told me the women earned 10 cents a bushel but the men earned 25 cents. She looked at me and said that was not right. I can testify she could work rings around a man.—Joy Frerichs

Daddy left on a day when the snowball bush, large blue-gray clusters of flowers, was in full bloom. Katie worked her body into the huge bush and watched as Mama attacked him with her fingernails, leaving marks on his left cheek, accusing him of hating his little family, especially her. Daddy drove away in his pea-green Plymouth Valiant. Katie remained in the bush at the mercy of Mama.

On any given evening, Mama could be found at the kitchen table, staring at her reflection in the dark windows, alone, the craziness growing. Her hair went from light brown to gray in one year. And instead of coloring the gray, she wore it like a war medal, referring to it as white. The price of her marriage. Mother and daughter lived on Black Mountain in a small house toward the bottom that had once belonged to Katie's grandmother, a woman who did well for herself by marrying a rich man.

Katie stayed with Mrs. Young, the old woman Mama hired to keep an eye on her after school while she went to work at the power company, where she made much less than the male employees and worked much harder.

"Remember, Katie, men are considered the best at anything they do, even if a woman can run rings around them."

"I will, Mama."

Mrs. Young made cookies every other day just for Katie—chocolate, oatmeal, and peanut butter. Her house smelled of old rose petals, and the rooms were crowded with furniture. Crocheted doilies covered the upholstered arms and backs of chairs and sofas. The den held the treasures, model horses of all kinds: pintos, stallions, quarter horses, and Katie's favorite, the appaloosa, gray as a sky loaded with rain. After all, the appaloosa was the most beautiful of horses. Grandmother had promised to buy Katie one as soon as she was old enough to take care of it alone. Mama wouldn't help. Katie had a name for this horse, Wind. Every afternoon Katie held the model horse and imagined what it would be like to own the real one. She had studied and knew all the steps of taking care of a horse. There was an old barn out back of their house and a paddock plenty big enough for Wind to roam. So Katie's letters to her grandmother were full of pleas to have the horse now instead of later.

⌁

Sometimes Mrs. Young forgot to pick Katie up from school, left her waiting until all the kids were gone. Finally, Katie would find her way to the mountain by following the road, just paved, to Mrs. Young's house. The first time this happened, the old woman cried when she understood that she had forgotten Katie, hugging her to her tiny bosom.

"You can't tell on me, Katie. Your mama will take you away from me. I love you too much. I promise I won't forget again."

Katie kept the secret.

⟡

A month before her eleventh birthday, a moving van came up the mountain road. The day was sunny and bright with the sparkle of cold in the air.

Mama stepped out the door onto the front porch. "Who are you looking for?" she yelled to the man who climbed from the truck.

"This is where Katie Owen lives? "

"Yes, but what do you want with my daughter?" Mama growled.

The man wore a green shirt with his name, Jack, embroidered above the pocket. He turned to Katie. "I am supposed to tell you happy birthday from your dad. He wishes he could be with you." He flashed an envelope in her face.

Katie took the letter. "Thank you." Red, green, and blue balloons dotted a card one would give to a five-year-old.

"What in the world?" Mama glared at Katie as if she had done something very wrong.

Daddy never could remember dates. He always mixed up her birthday. Mama always pointed out his mistake, rubbing salty accusations into the open wound.

The bike sat in front of her, gray and sleek, no baby look. A grown-up bike with a basket. Somehow she could let Daddy's forgetfulness go.

"Does he think you will forget what he did to us?" Mama watched Katie with owl eyes, demanding allegiance.

"I like my bike." Katie's voice was hard around the edges.

167

"What else could I expect out of you? You have always loved him no matter what." Now Mama glared at the bike.

"Lady, what do you expect the girl to do? This is a fine bike. All kids would like it." Jack winked at Katie.

"Aren't you finished?" Mama gave him a mean look.

"Just after you sign for this." He offered her a clipboard.

Mama grabbed it and scribbled her name.

Jack gave Katie a nod. "Enjoy that bike, young lady." He jumped in the truck and began turning around.

"You'd better be careful. Your daddy isn't here to buy your food and clothes. Instead, he sends a toy."

Shame soaked deep into Katie's bones. Her face flamed with heat as she climbed on the bike, kicked the stiff stand, wobbled somewhat from the large size, and shot in the direction of the road.

"Go ahead. Kill yourself. This mountain isn't made for bikes. You don't see other kids riding them."

When Katie reached the church cemetery, she jumped off to rest. Mrs. Young had said all of her family was buried toward the back, the older graves. A young girl with blonde hair stood in the back row, looking down at a grave. She was dressed a little weird, old-fashioned, but many families on Black Mountain didn't have a lot of money, much worse off than Katie and Mama.

The girl looked at her. "Who are you?"

"Katie Owen. I live down the mountain, almost at the bottom." Katie had never seen this girl at school.

"I like your bike. Are you rich?" She started walking toward Katie.

"Naw, my father sent this to me for my birthday next month."

"You're lucky. My daddy never had a pot to pee in.

That's what Mama always said, but she loved him better than any boy on this mountain."

"I think love is better than any amount of money. Don't you?"

The girl shrugged. "I don't know. I would have loved a lot of money."

"That's 'cause you got parents that love each other. You don't know what it's like for them to hate each other."

"That's true. My name is Mary Brown."

"How old are you?"

"Twelve."

"Do you go to school in the Gap?"

She shook her head. "Naw. Don't have to. Mama always taught me things. She was real smart, came from Asheville. Did a lot of book learning before she met my daddy."

"Wow, you're lucky. No school." Katie thought that had to be the best thing ever.

"Not really. I would have liked more friends. Kids always made fun of me."

It hadn't got past Katie how Mary talked about things as if they had happened to her long ago, but that didn't make a bit of sense. "Do you come up here to the cemetery much?"

Mary gave her a strange look. "I'm here a good bit."

"I'll come back to see you." Katie jumped on her bike.

"What is something you've always wanted?" Mary asked before Katie could leave.

"I want a horse. Not just any horse—an appaloosa. How about you?"

"A good friend." Mary looked real sad.

"I'll be back." Katie turned her bike in the direction of home. Mama would be mad she was gone so long.

❦

Katie waited until Mama left for work early one morning to pull out her bike. She had already decided to ride it to school. Mrs. Young hadn't picked her up in a couple of weeks, and this way she wouldn't have to walk the three miles to the mountain. The ride to school was smooth and much shorter than walking. She parked her bike by all the other bikes that belonged to the kids who lived in the Gap.

Winter in the North Carolina mountains came much quicker than other places. Way before Thanksgiving— sometimes even before Halloween—a fresh bed of snow would cover the grass. That afternoon when school let out, the wind had kicked up. Katie jumped on her bike and took all the neighborhood roads to avoid most of the cars. The sky was thick and gray. Wind blew her mousy hair from her face. The air caught its icy fingers around her lungs. She pumped and pumped, faster and faster, gaining distance, flying, joyful freedom, life off of Black Mountain. Maybe she could pedal straight into the sky, into the galaxy, into infinity. As the sky bled into the gray snow, lights blinked on through the windows of the houses, kids sitting at the dining table doing homework, moms washing dishes, laughing and talking. She pointed her bike toward home. Mrs. Young wouldn't even notice. She could go home.

Life in her house, if viewed from a large window by a bike rider, might have suggested order, dust-free tables, plastic slipcovers guarding Mama's precious furniture. Mama lounging in a bright red oversized chair. The light of the TV flashing like a store sign.

Katie was in the kitchen pulling steaks from the deep freezer along with a package of green beans when Mama's car tires crunched on the gravel outside.

"Katie," Mama screeched from the yard.

She tried to remember if she'd left her bike in the drive-way again, but no—she had put it behind the house so Mama would have nothing to fuss about. Katie went to the front porch. "What, Mama?"

"What the hell is that? What have you done?"

Katie looked in the direction of Mama's pointing. In the paddock was the most beautiful horse she had ever seen. The gray and spotted haunches told her she wasn't imagining what kind of horse stood there. "That's an appaloosa, Mama. I haven't done anything."

"I'm asking you how did it get there? Was it here when Mrs. Young dropped you off?"

Katie never paused. "No." She was telling the truth, but of course Mrs. Young had never dropped her off.

"We can't have a horse here." Mama still stood in the drive.

"Why? I'll take care of it. I know how," Katie begged.

"Don't be silly. We can't have a horse. We couldn't feed it." Mama began walking to the house. "We'll call the sheriff and see what he thinks."

Katie wanted to beg, to scream, but she remained silent.

"I hope your father hasn't done this. We don't have the money to take care of a horse." Mama looked at Katie. "What are we having for supper?"

"Steaks and green beans."

"Sounds good. I'll take mine well done." She went inside.

Katie followed her and headed to the kitchen.

"I'm going to call Mrs. Young and see if she saw the horse or if she knows who owns it."

"You don't have to do that." Katie stood close to the wall phone.

"You don't want me to call Mrs. Young? What's going on?" She pushed past Katie to the phone. "Mrs. Young, this is Katie's mom. Katie Owen." She frowned. "Did you see the horse by our barn when you brought Katie home?"

Katie put the frozen steaks in the frying pan, turning the gas up high. From where she stood, she could just make out the horse's long grayish white tail, swishing back and forth.

"Why in the world would you buy Katie a horse?" Mama's voice cracked.

For one silent moment, Katie thought everything would be ok.

"Your mother told you Katie wanted one?" Mama had a wild look on her face. "Your mother can't be alive, Mrs. Young. What are you talking about?"

The only sound was the steak sizzling, burning around the edges, raw in the middle.

"Mrs. Young, we cannot keep this horse. You must come get it. Take it back and get your money. My daughter cannot have a horse. And Mrs. Young, we will no longer need your services. Please come get this horse. If it gets out during the night, this will be your problem." Mama placed the phone in the receiver. "She's more of a nut than me. Fix me some whiskey, Katie. Don't you dare go around that horse out there. How are we going to get that woman to come get the horse? She says her mother, Mary, came to visit and said it was the one thing you wanted most in the world besides your father to come home."

Katie thought of the letter that had arrived earlier in the month with a return address in Asheville. Daddy had told her to call him if she needed to leave. In her yard was the horse she had always wanted. Of course they couldn't keep an animal. Mama could barely take care of the two of them.

"Get me a pink pill to go with the whiskey. Do not go around that horse."

The steaks burned, smoking. Katie turned off the flame and walked back to her room, where she had hidden the letter, and then went out the back door toward the paddock. She ran her hand through the appaloosa's mane.

"I'm sorry I can't keep you. I want you so bad. You'll make someone a good horse." For a minute she thought she might ride away on the horse, but that would cause more trouble. Mama was sure to find them both. In that moment, she knew what to do.

The crisp, cold air filled her lungs, taking away her breath, but still she pedaled, pedaling for her life through the frigid air, pedaling until the last possible second as Mama's voice cut through the dark from the front porch. Begging Katie home. Promising her the horse. Katie took the long way through the Gap, knowing all roads led back to the beginning. Only fifteen miles to Asheville. She pedaled with all her might. Katie raced the wind.

Part Three

Women to Be Reckoned With

THE DANCE LESSON

1935

This is not really an "issue," rather a testament to her grit and fearlessness. My paternal grandmother, who was born in 1904, was postmistress of the Willmathsville post office in the 1930s–1940s in Northeast Missouri. At that time, Willmathsville was a thriving, rural farming village. For many of those early years she delivered the mail on horseback to folks in town and the surrounding area.
—Mary Beth Kosowski

During the Depression, my maternal grandmother quit school to work on her family's farm. She worked in the fields alongside her brothers, but her main job was hitching the horses to the wagon because she could do it better and faster than the boys could.—Cindy Pope

The year was 1935 when Mama moved us to Black Mountain, North Carolina. I had just turned fifteen years old, and until our move, my whole life was Atlanta. Nothing about me, or Mama for that matter, was used to mountain living. Nothing. The only open land I'd known was Granny's backyard garden that she planted each spring so we wouldn't starve to death. The folks who had been well off were now just like everyone else, poor and struggling. Not a job existed. Daddy left three years earlier when things started going downhill. We hadn't heard a word from him. When word came from Granny's sister on Black Mountain that the post office needed someone to deliver mail on the mountain, Granny begged Mama to take this chance. And she did, dragging me right along. Her one and only daughter, Jean. Of course Mama got the job. How could they turn her down? She was smart as a whip and not afraid of a thing. Even when they told her she had to ride a horse to deliver the mail, Mama didn't blink. That's how we settled in Swannanoa Gap, the town at the foot of Black Mountain.

I can't say I loved school, but I didn't hate it either. There were no enemies to speak of except Mary Ann, but a lot of the kids didn't like her. I was the new girl from the city who didn't fit in with the locals. And my limp didn't help any. Mama said it was barely noticeable, but she was my mom and had to say things like that. Plus, she felt responsible because I was born early with my feet first. Breech is what she called it. I looked the word up and found out it meant, among other things, the lower part of anything. And having my limp was lower than low. When the doctor pulled me from Mama's womb, he dislocated my leg from the hip joint. By the time anyone knew, it was way too late to fix, assuming they could have at all. Thus the limp. Mary Ann was the one at school that made fun of me.

"Hopalong," she'd say, and laugh at her joke. The other kids did too. So I got a new name.

I had one friend, James Riley Jr. His family owned a hog farm right outside of town. He got teased all the time but he was like a duck, water just rolled off his back. Every day he waited on me under the big oak out in the schoolyard so we could walk home together.

One sunny day, James actually spoke to me. Lord, we never really spoke other than the niceties.

"I got to go home today at lunch to help hitch the horses. You want to come? Mama will make us something to eat." He gave me a goofy smile.

"I guess." I sure didn't smile at him.

❧

When Mr. Robbins, the teacher, rang the lunch bell, I followed James out of the schoolhouse, swinging my lunch pail beside me. Wasting food was a pure sin, and if nothing else, I'd feed it to the birds on the way to James's house. Why was I going to this boy's house anyway? Mama would make a fuss about me taking off without her knowing where I was at, but she didn't know what I did anyway. And I sure wasn't going because James acted goofy around me, which meant only one thing. He liked me in a way I did not like him. But I couldn't hurt his feelings. The other kids called him smelly, but he didn't stink a bit. Still, his house might. I got myself ready for this.

Mrs. Riley smiled real big when she saw me come in the door with James. "You didn't tell me you were bringing a friend. How nice." She was real pretty with blonde hair that made me think of a movie star.

James's cheeks turned pink. "This is just Jean, Ma."

"Oh goodness, your mama is the new postmistress. I seen her riding that horse up the mountain every day. She is pretty good."

"Yes ma'am. We're really happy because Mama needed the money pretty bad."

"Don't we all, honey." Mrs. Riley looked at James. "Got to hitch them horses. All four wagons. It's going to take all of them to haul those hogs to market."

That was when I realized nothing smelled. Not the yard or the house and certainly not Mrs. Riley. The house was pretty with lace doilies here and there. She was neat as a pin

179

in her blue dress and matching shoes. Kids at school had never been to the Rileys' home, or they wouldn't have made up such stupid lies.

"Come on with me, Jean," James called.

"James, a girl might not enjoy hitching wagons." Mrs. Riley gave me a soft look.

"I don't mind at all. I'm trying to learn all kinds of things," I answered politely.

"That's a good thing, Jean. Living on a farm requires its women to know many things that other women don't know." She gave me a knowing smile. Problem was I didn't know what she knew.

I followed James out the side door.

"I'll watch you do the first one, then I can help you with the other three," I offered.

He gave me a real odd look. "Have you ever hitched horses before?"

"No, but I can do anything. I'm like my mom."

"You need to know a little about horses first."

"What do I need to know? I'm just fastening them to the wagon."

His laugh stung. "Because if they sense you don't know what you're doing, they will bolt. Then my ass will be in real trouble for letting a girl that don't know anything about horses mess with the hitch."

"I'm smarter than you think," I shot back as we entered the large barn. Part of me understood that the Riley Family Farm was doing well when others were losing everything. For one thing, there were a lot of horses, and the barn was large and modern.

"You ain't farm smart because you ain't never lived on a farm."

"I'll prove to you I can do anything."

He raised his eyebrows. "Okay, but you better not mess up."

"I won't."

I watched him walk out two horses, talking to them, rubbing their sides when he placed the harnesses on them. He backed them close to a wagon, again talking in a low voice the whole time. He buckled and hooked.

"You want to stand and hold this horse while I do the next one?"

The whole process seemed easy enough. "I want to try."

"Okay." He sounded anything but trusting of my abilities. "First we get the horse."

I followed him into the barn.

"You have to come at them from the front. They don't know you."

When I entered the stall, the horse gave me a look that was pure human. And he wasn't encouraging me to come closer.

"Talk to him," James suggested.

"What do I say?"

He gave me a "I told you so" look. "Pretend Lucky, here, is a sweet dog. Pet him and talk to him."

"A really big dog." But I wouldn't show my fear. Lucky's neck was smooth like velvet. "You're soft, aren't you." Out of a need to be closer, I rubbed my cheek against his warm skin. Lucky leaned his head closer.

James handed me the harness. "Show me what you learned watching."

I had to prove myself. In a couple of minutes I had the harness fastened and ready to go.

James nodded. "You're good for having just watched."

181

His praise brought a warmness to my cheeks.

We worked together, and soon all the horses were hitched to the wagons.

A sandy-haired boy I'd seen many times at the gas station in town walked up to us. "You guys are finished? I came to help."

"Didn't need any help. Jean here is a quick learn, especially seeing she's a city girl from Atlanta." James grinned at me.

The sandy-haired boy smiled and held out his hand. "Nice to meet you, Jean. I'm Carlton McGuire. My dad owns the gas station. I think you and your mom are living in my granny's old house. Your mom does Dad's books for the gas station for rent."

My cheeks heated. How did I not know this?

"Dad says she is really smart. She's good at delivering the mail too. Gets on that horse without a bit of fear. You take after her." He gave me a wink.

"We got to eat, Jean, and get on back to school." James's voice was strained.

What had she done?

"Come by the gas station this afternoon and I'll give you a soda in the bottle." He looked at James. "You too, James."

"Sure."

⋘

When school was out, I shot out the door.

"Hey, where you going, Jean?" James trotted to catch me.

"I'm going to get my free soda. I haven't had one in forever."

182

"I could buy you one any time you want," James offered with a boastful voice.

"I'm not looking for handouts." A pressure built in my chest. Who did he think he was? Was he going to go and spoil us being friends?

"I'm going with you. He told me to come along too."

We got off the school bus in town instead of riding to the base of the mountain. I knew I was going to have a nice long walk home. So was James.

"I'll get one of the horses to give you a ride home from my house. Don't worry." James was reading my mind. I wasn't so sure I liked him acting that way.

"Ok, but I can walk."

We stood in front of the station. Carlton held the nozzle in one hand, pumping gas into a car. A greasy rag hung from his back pocket.

"Hello." James nudged me. "What you looking at?" He followed my stare before I could turn my head. "Carlton's nothing special, Jean. He dropped out of school thinking he'd join the army, but his daddy threw a fit. Said he needed him around the station. You know his mama is crazier than a bedbug."

"Crazy? What do you mean?"

"They have to keep her locked in the house. She hears voices no one else hears. Girls don't want to date him because of it. They're afraid his mama will kill them in their sleep. Before Carlton quit school, his mama showed up in her slip to walk him home. Well, you can guess what the kids did."

I couldn't even imagine what it would be like for such a thing to happen. Mama was the most solid person I knew.

"Sometimes she still gets out. It's hard to keep a lookout

for her all the time."

Carlton noticed us and threw his hand in the air. "You came after your soda. Hold on and I'll get it." He finished filling the car and replaced the pump handle. He looked at me again. "If you want a ride home, you can wait around for a little while. I'll drive you." He reached in his pocket and threw me a set of keys. "You can wait in the car."

The keys were warm with the heat of his hand. "Thanks."

"I'll ride with you too, Carlton," James said, giving me a look I couldn't quite read. He took the keys from me and led me to the car.

Carlton came to the car soon after we got in. James made sure I sat in the back. Carlton handed me a Coke over the seat. "He made you sit in the back." But his face was delighted, happy to be driving. When he pulled the car on the road, he looked over at James. "Jimmy boy, I want to go fishing Saturday. He turned to look at me. "Do you want to go too?"

Fishing. I'd never fished in my life. "I guess. I'm up for learning new things." I took a long swig of the Coke. It burned all the way down.

"If you come to the station tomorrow, I'll give you another soda and a ride home."

⁊

By the time Carlton and James dropped me off, we had decided to meet at the lake. And that's how it went. I finally had real friends. Boys, but friends all the same. Carlton called us the misfits. But there wasn't nothing that suggested he didn't fit in. We met each Saturday morning for fishing.

One morning maybe four Saturdays later, we were in a routine. The boys were at the water fishing, and I was on a blanket reading *Jane Eyre*, which was my habit instead. A flash of white at the tree line caught my eye. The figure was gauzy, floating, almost unreal, a ghost. But this person had real hair, long flowing hair, red as the dark red of dogwood trees in the fall, brilliant. She wore a white slip that did nothing to hide her breasts. Her walk was unearthly. I held my breath. The apparition put her finger to her blood-red lips. She wore a faraway expression. She was beautiful. Something about her smile suggested she wasn't really there with me, but somewhere else in a world of her own making. Her walk, silent, attracted no attention. Closer and closer. I closed my eyes.

The woman's hair brushed my face. She smelled of soap and powder. "I was once in love." The whisper was soft.

I opened my eyes and looked straight into the greenest stare.

"What are you doing?" Carlton's anger echoed across the water. He seized the woman's wrist.

"No!" The word came from somewhere deep inside the woman.

Carlton pulled the woman to the path cutting through the woods.

"She wasn't hurting me," I called.

James stood beside me. "That's Carlton's limp. We all have one, Jean. Mine is a family who owns a hog farm. We all have something."

Carlton didn't come back.

⁊

185

Two weeks later, Mama came home from work talking about a dance that was being organized for the Red Cross. Everyone was invited.

"I don't have anyone to go with."

"Of course you do. That nice James. I know he will want to go."

"He's just my friend."

"Who said friends can't go to dances together. Ask him."

Mama had no idea what she was getting me into.

Friday came and the dance loomed. Still I hadn't told James. Who knew what happened to Carlton. I hadn't seen him since he pulled his mama away from the lake. Finally, at the end of the day, I walked up to James.

"I'm going to the dance tonight. I'm going because by gosh I deserve to go as much as anyone. Mama said I should ask you to go too."

His face softened. "I can't dance. I don't think I'm the one you want to go."

"I need a friend. I can't dance a step, James. Everyone will make fun of my limp worse than ever. But I'm not missing this dance. It would break Mama's heart. She went and spent money on a new dress. Plus, if I skip this dance, for the rest of my life I will let others decide what I can or cannot do."

"I'll look like a fool." James looked at the ground.

"So will I, but I'm going. Meet me at the gas station. Please."

"Okay."

∽

I wore my new pink dress covered with delicate rosebuds, belted in the middle to show off my tiny waist. It was sleeveless, but I wore a white sweater buttoned at the top. I spied James, both hands shoved down in the pockets of his dress pants. Carlton stood close by with his foot on the fender of his car. James's shoulders were hunched as if bracing himself for a storm, while Carlton ran his fingers through his hair and laughed at something James said.

The road under my feet was packed dirt that would change to soup in upcoming rainy months. The sky that evening was a brilliant blue, and I drank in the color of the trees.

"There you are." James straightened his back and pulled his hands out of his pockets. "I was afraid you would back out." His eyes were alive with light.

Carlton whistled. "Boy, I wouldn't have known who this girl was. Look at you."

"Thanks."

Carlton opened the door to the car. "I'm taking you guys. Might as well check out this dance." I slid to the middle and James got in on the other side.

The dance hall was just a ways down the street. When I stepped from the car, a wave of dizziness swept over me. James took my hand. Adults and kids stood crowded at the door.

"I don't think I can dance," James muttered.

"I have to do this. Don't ditch me now."

The crowd began to move. There stood stupid Mary Ann with Rodney Marks of course. She gave me a frown. I held my gaze on her. She would not take this dance from me.

Inside the dance hall, James went straight to the punch bowl. And there I stood. The stupid cripple that no one liked, whose mama was the postmistress that delivered mail by horseback on the haunted mountain.

Carlton touched my shoulder. "We're going to dance, Miss Logan."

I shook my head. "I don't even know how."

"Yes you do. Just listen to the music. You can do this. My mom gave me lessons when I was young before." He guided me onto the floor as the band began to play a slow song. "This is the easiest kind of dancing. Come close." He put his arm around my waist and pulled me to him. "Stop thinking about your limp, Jean. Just move to the music. Follow me."

The music twisted and swirled around the room, around me, through me. Was it dancing or just mimicking? I wasn't sure if what I was doing was even right. We danced each song without stopping for a break. Once I saw James, and he winked at me as if to say, you're doing it. Carlton twirled me to a fast tune, and I was lost in the freedom of the music. I was free. I was normal. I was every bit as good if not better at dancing as Mary Ann. I was whole.

At that moment, the door to dance hall swung open. Carlton's mother floated in, wearing the same transparent slip as the day at the pond. "I'm here to dance. I love to dance. No one wants me to dance anymore."

The entire crowd took a breath at the same time.

"Play a slow song," she ordered.

Mary Ann put her hand on her hip. "Someone needs to do something about her. Look how she's dressed."

Carlton released me. He looked at his mother as if seeing her for the first time, and an idea came over his face.
"Could the band play a two-step?" he called. He took his
mother in his arms. The music began and everyone stepped
back. Carlton led his mother around the floor as she leaned
her head back, eyes closed. The couple moved in complete
grace. That's when I finally released my limp and all my ex-
cuses that kept me from living the life I wanted. I captured
the rhythm of the crazy woman's steps, took James's hand,
and led him around the dance floor.

❦

Carlton drove me to the train station when I left for college
in New York. Little did I know it would be the last time we
saw each other. He was killed on Highway 40 when a man
crossed the line doing eighty. James married a sweet girl,
even though Mrs. Riley had her heart set on me becoming
the daughter she never had. Mama finally got a truck to deliver mail on the mountain, and Granny came to live with
her once the war began. Me, Jean Logan, became a writer
after I graduated from college and stayed in New York,
where I worked for a big newspaper. At night I worked on
my own book about a boy and his mom. Carlton's mom still
slipped out of her house to dance in the streets and fields.
Mama would always mention her in the letters she wrote.
And I never forgot it was her that taught me to dance my
own way, be the woman I was meant to be.

A SPIDER'S BITE

1941

My mother, who grew up in Mexico and received Red Cross training, wanted to be a nurse. Her brother told their parents that seeing naked bodies would be bad for her reputation, so they would not allow her to study nursing. Instead, she became one of the first air hostesses for PanAm Mexico. They didn't know what they wanted from the air hostesses. Her Red Cross training, fluency in six languages, charming and intelligent personality, and poise won her the job. During her time on this job, she met John Wayne, Cantinflas (Passepartout in Around the World in 80 Days), danced a waltz with Walt Disney, and was subtly propositioned by the president of another Central American country. Eventually she married an American Air Force flight navigator (my dad), moved to Georgia, raised nine amazing children, and co-owned/managed a nuclear laundry.—Cathy Benedetto

The lavender scent that hung heavy in the air and the way the room turned ice cold like January in July told me Mama was back. The summer she took to haunting me was so hot I thought I'd die just walking across the room. The days stretched out to a never-ending spot on the horizon. Black Mountain should have been more tolerable than other places stricken by the drought. All I could do was dream of leaving home, putting that mountain in my dust. It all started when I took a Red Cross training in Asheville and got it in my head that I was going to be a nurse, offer my services in the war over in Europe. Do something exciting. When I made this announcement at supper one night, Robbie, my stupid older brother, told Daddy it would be a pure sin for me to be any such thing.

"Just think of all the naked soldiers she'll have to treat. Mama would be rolling over in her grave."

Mama wouldn't have cared one bit. Mama would have wanted me to be something as noble as a nurse.

"Jeannie Ray, you ain't leaving this mountain and going into any war." And things went just like that. Daddy crumbled my hopes just like the big square of cornbread that he crumbled into his milk.

"You got to find you a man, a husband that can control you." Robbie wiped his greasy fingers on his pants instead of the napkin.

"Why don't you shut up and find you a wife, you big dummy," I yelled. Of course, this sure didn't make me seem any more grown up.

Orb weaver spiders work on their intricate webs with one thing in mind: to capture their prey.

I figured Mama showed up at that time because my own spirit was bumping into every wall in our little house, or maybe it was because of Maynard Connor, forced to come home from being a carnival boy after he broke his leg saving a little old woman from a runaway elephant. I took one look at that man out at Daddy's still, turning a bottle up, and wondered if I could make him work for me. He'd left the mountain for a good amount of time. Maybe he was my answer. I'd spent enough time looking through Mama's eyes to figure out that she pulled the whole load on our farm. Though a person can't really know a thing without walking in another person's shoes. Mama's shoes were awful big.

Once, Mama had big dreams. We'd sit on the porch in the evening, just me and her, talking about how one day we'd have a fine new home and so many clothes we'd run out of places to put them all. We had to find the money somehow, or as Mama said, our ship had to come sailing in. The only problem with this thought was that the ocean was way out of reach. And then a blood clot—aneurysm was the word the doctor used—stopped Mama in the field, and all her dreams melted away into that dry ground. It was the worst crop we ever had. When I found Mama, she was already cold, staring at the sky with a blank look. That night I dreamed about a spider, a black one, weaving a web of the biggest kind in the corner of the room. The thing gave me a thought, put it right in my head. *Lots of work catches your prey.*

Mama's spirit could be calming, and when it was, I wrapped myself up in her and relaxed a little. Daddy, he didn't even notice. He was so full of shine it had turned him inside out.

"You got your head in the clouds, girl. A good swift kick in the ass would bring you right back to earth." He laughed at his corn-liquor wisdom.

The next day Daddy made it in for lunch, which was real unusual since he was on a liquid diet. "Maynard is a fine boy," he said. "He can drink just like a man. He's done got himself so many girls he can't keep count. Fine boy if you ask me."

Mama got all stirred up over that comment, seeing how she knew who one of the girls pining for him was. Her favorite serving dish jumped right off the counter to the floor.

"How in the sam hill did that happen?" Daddy looked at me like I caused the whole thing.

But I didn't worry none. I had leaving on my mind. Anyway I could find.

Maynard worked on the next farm over for poor Widow Bryson. Her last name came from a city in the Smoky Mountains, and she was way too young to be a widow. Mr. Bryson got himself killed in a poker game. Folks all over the mountain worried over Maynard, but they had no need. He visited Polly Riley every day too. She was named after her great-great-grandmother who was full-blooded Cherokee. And like her great-great-grandmother she was considered the prettiest girl on Black Mountain. Polly's daddy done told her she couldn't marry anyone that didn't have land and worked hard. He planned on taking her to the reservation as soon as she finished her book learning so she could meet a good Cherokee boy.

That Maynard had two females drooling after him and no telling who else. But I saw him as the one to rescue me from my drab life on the mountain. Lord, I didn't no more love him than there was a man in the moon eating cheese. One man was just as good as the next. Maynard would come around to my way of thinking when Polly's daddy finally ran him off for good. I was real patient. Waiting was no problem for me. I'd learned how to lay still each night in my bed, so Daddy would think I was asleep. Some nights it took him hours before he passed out. I wasn't so good at ignoring Mama's spirit sweeping around my room, all frantic like a bunch of hornets after a rock hit their hive. Hornets are the meanest insects alive. They don't know how to give up until they find something or someone to plant their stingers in. Mama was stirred up about something.

Many orb weavers build a new, elaborate web every
day. They'll begin work on it as the sun is going down.
By morning they go off to rest with a finished web
waiting on its catch.

The next morning after I set my eyes on Maynard, Shirley the two-headed doctor—that was a person who conjured spells—came knocking at our door. Most folks were right scared of Shirley. Daddy said she could charm the soul out of a person, and he stayed clear of her. He was already gone from the house when she showed up. Me, I wasn't no more afraid of her and her so-called magic than I was of Mama's sweet spirit. If the truth be told, nothing much scared me except a life with a drunk daddy and a no-good lazy brother. That wasn't good Christian thinking, but God knew my thoughts and we were fine, me and him.

Shirley stood on our front porch, one hand on her hip, the other pulling at her curly black hair. She was right pretty with her copper-colored skin...until she opened that mouth of hers. All her front teeth were gone or rotting, and the words that came out were sometimes fouler than her breath.

"Hi Miss Shirley, what brings you to see me?" I smoothed my apron.

"Jeannie Ray, your mama is about to drive me slap out of my mind."

I had the urge to laugh in her face. My mama wouldn't have been caught dead at Shirley's house, but I was good at acting. I thought once I got off the mountain I'd ditch Maynard and get myself on a stage somewhere. So I stood right there waiting like the spider I'd seen spinning her web outside my window the evening before. The threads full of dew sparkled that morning. That one little spider worked all night on the details, knowing full well one puff of wind could destroy her trap, and she would have to start again.

"Your mama is hell-bent on you learning spells. Says you'll need them in your life."

"That's the nicest thought, Miss Shirley, but I'm not a bit interested. I got me some plans, and I ain't going to need any old magic."

"Jeannie Ray, I wish it was up to me, but it just ain't. Your mama's done thrown her a big old fit at my house one too many times in the last few days. I'm going to honor her wishes if for no other reason than to get her the hell out." She narrowed her eyes to slits, and her stare just dared me to think otherwise. "And if you think all that sliding up to Maynard Connor is going to get you somewhere, you're dead wrong. He has an eye for the ladies, and he don't care which one. I'm here to tell you that. He ain't never leaving this mountain again. His mama is here and is getting on in age."

"How you know so much about him?"

"That's not a bit of your concern. He's just a mountain boy. Never leaving Black Mountain for long. Just stay away from him. You're young and don't need the likes of him."

I thought I might just throw me a big old fit and chase her away, but something inside said maybe throwing spells would work for me. I might find me some of that wisdom the spider owned. "When do you want me to start learning?"

Shirley smiled real big. "Your mama's going to be right proud of you."

"You know my daddy doesn't tolerate magic."

"Just leave him to me." She leaned in close. "You'll be the boss when you learn to conjure, Jeannie Ray. Of course you have to use magic for the good of others. Ain't no place on the mountain for someone who uses spells for their own good." She winked like we had some kind of special shared knowledge.

"Who taught you spells?"

"My mama was colored and my daddy was white with lots of money, real big in the city where I was birthed, New Orleans. His mean old wife ran Mama out of town. She was fearful we'd steal something she'd lost a long time before. Mama had the last say by hexing that mean woman. But you see, all that was caused by my daddy. That's what men are good for, Jeannie Ray. They're not worth a plug nickel. All they're good for is hanging them out on a limb over a churning river just to watch them squirm. Of course, they be all right to cuddle to on a cold winter night. That's if you keep your mind and don't go having your soul wrapped up in them. Anyway, my mama taught me her hoodoo and that's what I'm going to teach you." She gave me another smile. "Hoodoo is a little this and some of that, and a big bunch of the other thrown in just for fun." She laughed so hard she grabbed her side.

"I'm not so sure I need all that."

"Might as well learn it all. You're learning from one of the best." She turned to leave. "I'll see you at dawn tomorrow. Come to my place so I don't have to deal with that daddy of yours. We got a bunch of work to do."

When Daddy came home later that evening, he had a burr up his butt. "I don't have no tolerance for spooks or such, Jeannie girl." He took him a long swig off his bottle.

"You smell that?" Lavender filled the air real strong.

"All I smell is cabbage and pinto beans. Damn, I'm sick of beans."

I imagined that whole pot of beans spilling over his head. "If I had more money I could make better food." I'd heard Mama say the same thing many times.

A flash of light lit up the room, and salty blood filled my mouth. I took a couple of steps back and touched my lip. "I'm going to learn some magic from Shirley."

"By God, you won't. The likes of her ain't coming around my place."

"I guess you can tell her yourself." I moved out of reach.

"You ain't got a lick of sense just like your mama, just about worthless. I won't have you messing around with that two-headed woman."

"You go tell her that to her face." I looked at him with all my hatred.

Fear flickered across his face. "Give me my food."

That night Mama came and stood at the end of my bed. Her beautiful face was free of all the lines. A daisy was tucked in her honey-colored hair. She opened the fingers of her left hand. On her palm sat the spider. The one I saw building its web. "Look at the details, Jeannie Ray. You got to get all the details." She smiled pretty-like, closed her fingers over the spider, and turned away, walking right through the wall.

The Cherokee believe that the first fire was brought to the earth on the back of a spider. The spiders were teachers and protectors of wisdom.

The world was gray and soft like a newborn kitten sleeping in a ball when I scooted out the door without Daddy even stirring.

Shirley was waiting just like she promised, standing on her front porch with her hand on her hip. "You seen your mama last night."

"Yep."

"She warned you."

"I guess you could say it was a warning. She had a flower in her hair."

"What kind?" Shirley balled her fingers into a fist and relaxed them again.

"A simple daisy."

She took a step back. "Lord, don't you understand a thing? I thought you were smarter than that."

"A flower is a flower. I don't see what all the fuss is about."

"I got to start from the very beginning with you. Daisies are the oldest flowers in the world."

"And what do you know about the world?" I wanted to laugh.

"I know daises are considered the flowers of sight. They let a person see better, real clear. Your mama wants you to see something. Did she say anything?"

"I don't see what a daisy has to do with it."

"She's telling you Maynard ain't a bit good for you."

"How do you figure that?"

"Who is the one here that knows magic? Let's get to work."

And that we did. She started with simple things like seeing visions in clear, still water and love spells that would be useless to me. But I learned all Shirley showed me. In the meantime, I watched Maynard from afar as my simple plan formed.

One afternoon a good ways into our learning, I was on my way home from Shirley's when I saw Polly and Maynard sneaking out to the schoolhouse that was a church on Sundays. I was thinking about how magic was a funny kind of power that could be released better than harnessed. I peeked through the window. There they were, all over each other

199

close to the pulpit. Talk about daring God. Maynard kissed
Polly and touched her behind. I swallowed a laugh. When
he started unbuttoning her dress, I left for home. That wasn't
something I wanted to see. Someone needed to save Polly
from her own bad decisions. Yep, a spell had to be made. I
picked me some daisies in one of the meadows and scattered
the petals all over my bed when I got home. Then I wrote
Maynard's name a hundred times and folded the paper ten
times. I put it under my pillow.

Around sundown, here came Maynard rumbling down
the dusty road. He looked here and there as if he were killing
time rather than heading home. That's how he noticed me
standing on the porch.

"Well, Miss Jeannie Ray, you're a sight to linger on."

I just smiled, trying not to think of Polly and any of the
other girls. "I've been waiting on you. I need you to come fix
my bed. One of the ropes broke. Daddy, well, you know how
he is."

"You ok, Jeannie Ray?" His smile was real smooth, and
I understood why the widow had thrown him out for turning
her down.

"I'm fine, Mr. Connor. I've been dying to get that old
bed fixed. It's so saggy."

He took a step back like he sensed the danger around
him. "Why you out here all by yourself? Where's your
daddy?"

I touched his arm real soft. "I knew you'd be by, and he's
off somewhere drinking like always."

"You be real pretty, Jeannie Ray. What's different about
you?"

"I think it's because I've learned just what I want."

"What's that?"

"Oh, I've learned how to throw a few spells. Do you know anything about conjuring spells?"

"I ain't much of a believer in magic." He gave a half grin.

I was only inches from his face.

He stared down at my lips. "You going to get yourself kissed if you ain't careful."

The smell of strawberries was on his breath. "My kisses are spells."

"Why you want to put a spell on me?"

I counted to ten in my mind. "I'm aiming to leave here, Maynard." I was a spider weaving my web. Why, in only a few minutes I could weave several rows of fine sparkling thread, around and around and around. I wasn't even going to need my bed for this spell. I opened my fingers and brushed that spider real gentle. I could have sworn she smiled as she crawled down his shirt, as if we were one and the same. He kissed me.

Orb weavers signify that we are the engineers of our own destiny. Catch your dreams and make them happen.

Funny thing about spider bites is people sometimes don't even feel them. Maynard sent Daddy for me at the end of the next day.

"Maynard's in a real bad way. Says you put some kind of spell on him. The boy is talking out of his head. He wants you to come over to his mama's farm." Daddy frowned at me. "You didn't put no spell on him, did you?"

"You told me you couldn't tolerate conjuring."

He watched me to see if I needed a good smacking and nodded. "Go on over there and see if you can help settle him down."

Maynard sat on the front porch, white as a ghost and shivering like we'd done got our first snowfall. When he saw me, he gave me a long look. "Take this spell off me, girl."

"This ain't my spell."

"I'll do anything you want. What you want?"

"I ain't done a thing to you." I watched him close. "You give me the keys to your truck and twenty dollars, and I'll go fetch Miss Shirley. She's the only one who can remove a spell."

"She ain't going to help me none."

"Ain't my problem, Maynard."

He dug in his pocket, giving me a bill and the keys. "Be right careful with my truck."

"Sure I will."

I drove over to Miss Shirley's, where she stood on her front porch waiting on me like she knew I was coming.

"What you doing with Maynard's truck?"

"He gave it to me."

"I can't believe that."

"It's true."

"What you here for?"

"He's right sick. I think he might have got him a spider bite from one of those poison brown spiders. You know the kind."

"Oh Lord." Worry formed a frown on her face.

"He's talking out of his head. Said I put a spell on him. We both know I ain't that good."

"I'll go."

"I knew you would." I started the truck. "Oh Shirley, I'm just fed up with learning spells, but I do appreciate what you've taught me."

"You can't quit now. I'll see you tomorrow."

I backed up the truck. She was going to lay her hands on Maynard, and everything between them two would change. He would fall madly in love with her. My spell would work. They both would settle down and get married. Imagine them two scoundrels.

As for me, I took one last look at the mountain in the rearview mirror. I thought about how that spider's web was blowing real nice in the breeze, how she had moved on to a better place after biting Maynard. Me, I thought I might like to apply to a good nursing school. Then I could go to war and help the soldiers. Meet me some fine men. Go all the way to England and France. That's what I had a hankering for. A life full of adventure.

EBB TIDE

1968

After divorcing her abusive second husband in 1931, my grandmother was called a harlot because she remarried a mere five months after her first husband died. She would have received compassion and respect as a widow, but divorcing for any reason besides adultery was considered an unforgivable sin by the Primitive Baptist Church. The only way to be forgiven and allowed back into the church would have been to remarry the ex-husband who frequently beat her and then later tried to shoot her after he couldn't get her money out of the bank.—Jalane Rolader

My great-great-grandfather's sister Becky had three sets of twins born out of wedlock by the 1910 census, and she had three single births in between the twins. The truth is that she was more or less held in bondage to a married man after she came to work for his family. Her eldest son wound up killing the married man to free Becky, and a younger son took the murder charge because he was sixteen, which meant a lighter sentence. The younger son did ten years for manslaughter.—Anita Kendrick Bobo

Mary Jo smacked her gum and pulled Mama's hair so hard with the comb, tears came into her eyes. A cigarette burned in the ashtray in front of the mirror. Tally watched Mary Jo twist and weave Mama's long hair. Hers was next.

"Take it easy on my hair," Mama barked.

"I just wish you'd try some color. This gray would soak it up and you'd be years younger, Jodie. You're too darn young to look like an old woman."

"I don't care a thing about looking younger." Mama's face drew up like she was sucking on lemons.

"Don't you want a man, honey? You're too young to shrivel up and die like your mama did." Mary Jo smacked her gum.

"First, there ain't one man left on the mountain for a woman. Second, if I can't get a man without coloring my hair, then I don't one." Mama looked at Tally in the mirror. "Besides, what kind of example is that for my girl?"

Mary Jo clicked her tongue in disgust. "Lord, Jodie, no one is saying you have to give your life up just because you got a kid." She ran her fingers through Mama's hair. "This beautiful gray will look good on you thirty years from now. Right now you need to be a blonde like Marilyn Monroe. I just thought she was the prettiest when she sang happy birthday to the president. You're only thirty. Do something with your life."

Mama frowned. "I'm twenty-eight and you know it."

"See there. Your whole life is in front of you, girl." Mary Jo began to roll Mama's hair on little plastic rollers. "You need to forget this old-style permanent wave and tease it a little. Give yourself some height." Mary Jo wore her hair teased real high, and it was the most beautiful shade of red. "I've gotten so many comments on my hair, I've just quit counting." Mary Jo was the gossip in the Gap. If anyone wanted to know something they went to her. Sometimes they actually got the truth.

"I should think you have."

Tally knew that tone of voice. Mama disapproved of Mary Jo's hair.

"Do I hear a little high and mighty in your voice, Jodie?"

Mary Jo pulled Mama's hair hard again. Sometimes Tally wished Mary Jo could work some magic on Mama and turn her into a happy person again. "You need some fun, sweetie. You can't mope around forever."

Mama pulled her shoulders real straight like a proud Aztec queen—Tally had seen a drawing in her history book. "Tally and I are going on a real trip."

Mary Jo rolled her eyes at herself in the mirror. "Well la tee da, a real trip. You got more money than me." She made a face. "Sorry. I guess you still got some of that money from James. He was a good man. It's a doggone shame all our good men are being killed in that war."

"I don't want to talk about James. You know good and well Martin is taking us."

Mary Jo's face reflected exactly how Tally felt. "Jodie, when you going to learn to say no to that man? He ain't what you want. When I talk about men, I ain't talking about men like Martin. You heard what happened to Cathy's family, didn't you? She has horrible taste in men."

Mama gave her a long look. "No. I didn't hear. And don't go comparing me to someone who is sleeping with a married man."

"All her kids were born by that man. Him married and just carrying on with her like he's all that. I'm not sure she even had a choice, Jodie. Anyway, her eldest boy went and killed him, his own daddy. Told Cathy she was free now. The younger boy took the blame because he won't get as bad of a sentence being sixteen. Heard they were sending him to that hospital in Georgia. You know, that lunatic hospital. You need to be free of Martin. You can't keep letting him interrupt your life, not to mention how bad it is for sweet Tally here. The man ain't never going to settle into a real relationship." Mary Jo smiled.

Each roller in Mama's hair was tight and formed neat rows down the side of her head. "It's good for Tally to spend time with a father figure. I'm grateful for his time."

"God, Jodie. Wake up. Are you always going to be a doormat? You can't replace Tally's daddy. And Martin isn't the one to replace such a fine solider with."

"Martin is only the second man I've known," Mama admitted.

"Then live on the wild side, honey. Meet you a third man. Do like me—find a man with money and sweet love in his eyes."

Mama gave Mary Jo a frown. "And one foot in the grave."

"Better than what you have, sweetie." Mary Jo laughed without taking any offense.

Tally walked out of the shop into Mary Jo's front yard. She was a smart lady, using her front room for her business. A sign painted in pink sat near the road. The Hair Palace. The whole town thought it was the tackiest thing since the mayor painted the water tower black and white like a checkerboard. Mama and Tally lived on Black Mountain not far from the town. But mostly the mountain felt like a million miles away.

Tally wished she could live in Mary Jo's pink-trimmed house, close to everything else in town like the bakery and the Piggly-Wiggly. Daddy had promised they would have a little farm when he came home from Vietnam. Tally never thought he wouldn't come home. Now, during her spring vacation, Martin had decided to take "his girls" off to the coast. Tally had never seen the ocean and really wanted to visit the beach, but not with Martin.

◈

Early before light showed on the horizon, Martin knocked on the front door. Mama must have answered. Tally sat on her bed waiting to leave.

"Are you ready for our big trip?" Martin asked.

Tally imagined Mama, with her curls fluffed out around her head, standing at the door dressed to the nines, smiling at him.

"Well, mister, you look better than a paycheck with twenty hours of overtime."

"Give me a hug. You feel better than anything I could imagine."

And with that, Mama was swept into the magic Martin always brought into her life. This time he had a brand new Ford Mustang convertible. Mama was cooing all over it. Sometimes Tally didn't like this mama.

"Tally," Mama called. "Get your things and come on. It's time to leave."

As Tally crawled into the cramped backseat, Mama smiled, her face lit like a candle in the night. "It's going to take eight hours to get there. Why don't you go back to sleep? Time will fly by."

When Mama thought Tally was asleep, she began to talk to Martin. "Cathy Benson—we went to high school together, the one with so many kids—her oldest done went and killed his own daddy."

Martin didn't say a word.

"Killed him with a bullet from his own gun. The youngest is taking the blame because he is underage."

"Time won't be as long if he gets any at all," Martin said.

"She just let that man in anytime he wanted. She knew he was never leaving his wife." Mama was quiet for a minute before she went on talking. "Martin, are you staying this time?" Her voice tinkled like glass crystals on a chandelier.

"Remember, Jodie, we are living in the moment. No ties." Martin said this like he was talking to a kid.

"Yes."

"Let's have a good trip without muddying the water with your emotions."

"You're right, of course."

"I reserved a great motel on the beach. Tally will like the ocean. We'll all have fun."

Tally squeezed back hatred by closing her eyes so tight that lights danced in her mind like angry little fairies.

∽

Tally smelled the ocean long before she saw the water beating the shore, the wind whipping other sound from the air. The ground went from the red dirt of Georgia to white sand. And when she caught her first glance of the large body of water, her heart raced and she gripped her hands together.

"This is the marshes. We have to go over the bridge to the island. Then you see the real ocean." Martin gave her a wink in the rearview mirror.

Tall white birds stood here and there in the grass that waved in the wind.

Martin let the roof down, and Tally smelled a different world. Old history lived in the place. Tally was sure of it. She closed her eyes tight when they crossed the long, high bridge onto the island. Neither Mama nor Martin spoke. If the car careened off the side of the bridge into the water, what would happen? What would change in the world? But the new car remained straight, smooth, fast. Martin took them to a large pier. Tally forgot her hatred and jumped from the car and ran to the water to watch it rush into the sand. She kneeled and tried to catch the constant motion of the waves. Constant motion: roll in, relax, and pull back out into the ocean. Tally removed her shoes and touched the wet sand just as the water rushed around her ankles, sand pulling away, shifting under her feet. The wind blew so loud in her ears that no other sound was allowed inside her head. A bird glided on the breeze. The whole world existed within two feet of her. A flash of gray in the water stopped her thoughts. Again the flash, clearer, slick, graceful. She turned to yell at Mama, to point out the creature, but Mama was gone; only Martin stood in the place where she had been just before.

Tally turned back to the ocean, drawn and torn at the same time. The gray streak exposed a fin. A shark. Never had she thought of a shark as beautiful. The creature jumped in the air, twirled, and dove under. No, this couldn't be a shark. Her heart raced, and the roar of the wind smothered her call to Martin. She gathered her shoes and ran, climbing the stairs two at a time only to find Mama just behind Martin, a distance between them. And there is where her hatred lived, in the space between these two people.

"I thought I saw a shark, but it couldn't have been. This creature was too pretty."

Mama left for the car without speaking.

Martin smoked a cigarette, wearing a military outfit. Something Tally had just noticed. Had he been to war too?

"You saw a dolphin. They call them the angels of the sea."

This name moved through her. "Why?"

"Because they are so special. You can swim with them, and they won't hurt you."

"How do you know?" She found it hard to believe he was telling the truth.

"I swam with them."

Tally tried to imagine Martin in swimming trunks and no shirt. She giggled.

"What? You don't believe me?" He laughed too. "Me and my best friend came here. We swam with them together."

"You have a best friend?"

"Did." He said with a sad smile. "We knew each other from the time we were born. He lived next door to me my whole childhood."

"Where is he now?"

"He died." He opened the car door so Tally could get inside. "Come on, I'm going to take you to the motel. I want to change into my bathing suit."

I laughed. "I can't see you in a bathing suit."

Mama sat in the car. "Don't act silly, Tally."

"She's got to act silly, Jodie. She's twelve years old. It's what twelve-year-olds do best."

∽

The motel was pink, the color pink Mary Jo favored so much. Tally's heart lifted at the sight. Surely this was a good omen. The room was huge with two large beds, and Tally got one all to herself. She threw herself in the middle and stared at the ceiling as Mama busied herself in the large white bathroom. Over Tally's bed hung a scene of the ocean. She imagined she was alone away from the adults, frozen in time, in some other world. Mama came out, wearing her new bathing suit.

"Tally, get off that bed."

Tally stood. "When are we going to swim?"

Martin held up some bright blue swimming trunks. "As soon as I change."

Tally giggled as he shut the bathroom door.

"What is so funny, Tally?" Mama's words chipped at Tally's happiness.

Tally dug out her swimsuit. "Are you going to swim, Mama?"

"I'm going to sit on the beach. I never learned to swim. I don't like the water."

"I saw dolphins today. Martin told me that he swam with them and his best friend."

Mama's face turned sad.

"Did you know that his best friend from when he was born died?"

"Hush about that, Tally." Mama's voice had a shrillness that made Tally look in another direction, find something to concentrate on. The bedside clock. She watched the hands, trying to see one move.

∽

Mama sat on a quilt spread on the beach in the brilliant white sand. Tally ran into the ocean in her peach-color Catalina suit. Martin, smoking a cigarette, ambled from the quilt to the water's edge. The wind roared. The water moved with a rhythm. Something brushed her leg. She looked down and it was seaweed. The waves washed up to her waist and moved her whole body. More seaweed wrapped around the other leg. A burning began in the leg, then stabbing pain filled her body. Her scream was swallowed by the wind. Tally tried to move, but the pain owned her. Another scream, and she forced herself to move. Mama pointed at Tally, her face strained against the bright sun. Tally screamed again. This time the sound found a break in the wind and bounced in the air. Both Mama and Martin ran to the water.

"What is it? What happened?" Mama yelled.

Martin grabbed Tally from the water and placed her on the sand, grabbing a handful, grinding it into her leg.

"What are you doing? Are you crazy?" Mama screamed.

The pain began to fade. Big, angry red welts marked her leg.

"Jellyfish," Martin said.

"Does she need to go to the hospital?" Mama cried.

Martin carried Tally to the quilt. The pain faded more.

"No. I'm better. Martin made it go away."

Martin looked at Mama. "The sand works like meat tenderizer, softens the sting."

And in that moment, Tally knew Martin wasn't so bad.

"I told Mama about your best friend swimming with the dolphins with you. I wanted to try and find them."

He shook his head.

Martin left the motel room at dark with the spoken intentions of bringing them supper. Tally sat on the bed with her leg propped up on an extra pillow as she flipped the stations on the TV.

"I have some peanut butter crackers," Mama said.

"I'll wait for Martin to bring food."

"He won't be back."

Tally looked at Mama. "What do you mean?"

"I'll call Mary Jo tomorrow. Her and that old man of a husband will come for us. I know she will if for nothing else but to tell me 'I told you so.'"

"I'm not eating peanut butter crackers." Tally flung herself into a standing position. There was no pain.

"I'm sorry."

"I hate both of you."

"I don't talk about his best friend, Tally. It always makes him act crazy."

"Why?"

"His best friend was your daddy. They were both in the war but in different places. Martin came home. Your dad didn't."

Tally ran out the door. She was sure Mama would follow, but she didn't. She thought beyond hope that Martin would be there, grinning, holding bags of takeout. Instead, she found the ocean, still, withdrawn, pushed far out, the still line of a painting. The wind was gone. The air was heavy with heat. The deafening noise had disappeared. She ran to the beach in search of the dolphins. The sand was wet under her feet but no water flowed over them. She walked. The water had left her behind.

The sky was dotted with a thousand bright stars. Tally spun in circles, watching until she became so dizzy she fell and the world continued to reel. She lay on the wet sand in her good shorts outfit, wishing she could become part of the ocean that would roar back to shore and sweep her away.

"Are you ok, little girl?"

A bright light shown on her. "Yes."

"I thought you were dead, laying out here. The ocean

will come back in a few hours." A grisly old woman, holding a wire basket on a chain, sat on the sand beside Tally. "I'm going home. Can't do much crabbing in ebb tide."

"What's ebb tide?"

"You're a tourist." The old woman looked at the sand and then back at Tally. "It's when the ocean grows quiet and attempts to leave the shore. You'd better go on home. Your mama and daddy will be worried."

"My daddy is dead." Tally stood. "He can't worry." She turned and went back to the room.

Mama came and crawled in the bed with Tally. Martin didn't come back.

⁓

The next morning, Tally woke to beating on the door. Mama opened it and there stood Mary Jo.

"Lord, Jodie, what you got yourself into? Out here on this island. The damn wind is making a mess of my hair."

Tally stood and pulled the curtains open. The ocean rushed in and out, normal now.

"Thanks for coming." Mama began to gather their things.

"Will you take me up on that color? Start living a life now? You can't change what happened. It will always stand between you like a ghost following you from one place to the next. Ghosts don't always make themselves visible. Sometimes they just hang around tearing lives apart."

Mama looked at Tally and then at herself in the mirror. "You know, Mary Jo, I think I will, and I want me some of that red lipstick too."

Mary Jo's mouth hung open. "I'm speechless." She

216

looked around. "Let's go before Tony has a heart attack in the car. He dearly hates the heat and the ocean."

Tally turned back to the view through the window. The ocean had hurt her. But in that moment she knew she couldn't hate something so beautiful, constantly moving, changing, growing, and withdrawing. Inside her formed, if not an understanding, an acceptance for the differences that existed between life and the ocean.

A MOMENT OF LAUGHTER

1966

My maternal grandmother was accepted at prestigious Bellevue Teaching Hospital in New York for psychiatric nursing. But my grandfather proposed to her, and she had to choose between marriage and an incredible education opportunity a world away. The school didn't allow female students to be married. —Laura Sharpe Galluzzo

Note: This story is dedicated to all the women who lost who they were supposed to be due to the rules of society.

Lonnie was eighteen years, two months, and seven days old when he was called to serve his country. Our family was huge, three boys and two girls, not counting Grandmother Owen, who lived on the main floor in an apartment. Daddy and Mama went in debt to build this add-on for her privacy and ours. Of course, there was no such thing as privacy on Black Mountain. Everyone knew everyone and every move made. Grandmother Owen was a product of the mountain, generations mired in the history. Even if she stayed in her apartment half the time, I had the rest of the family filling up each empty space in the old farmhouse.

Lonnie was the oldest of the kids, and I was next in line, the oldest daughter. I wish I could say Lonnie and me were close, but nothing could be further from the truth. He committed all the crimes older brothers always think up against younger sisters. Before he graduated from Black Mountain

High, he was in three of my classes, which was horrible considering his popularity and the fact that only seventeen months separated our birthdays. I had no freedom of choice. He watched me like a hawk; he saw it as his job to make sure I was being a good girl and doing everything my parents expected out of me. He was captain of the football team and was always bringing friends home. If not for this, I wouldn't have gone to the junior/senior prom with Mark Young, one of the best hunks in school. It turned out real bad because Lonnie and Laura, my brother's girlfriend, hounded us the whole time, but Mark liked me, and this was a dream come true.

I have to admit I was proud of Lonnie when he wore his cap and gown. I couldn't come right out and say it. Brothers, especially older brothers, hate that kind of attention, and he would have used it as a weapon against me. But little did either of us know on that hot afternoon that Lonnie wouldn't be home much longer. As we stood on the high school's football field, the line of graduates walked between the rows of metal folding chairs. I stood at the end with the rest of the family right there with me. When Lonnie walked by, tall, straight, I reached out and touched the sleeve of his gown. He turned and looked at me. I was messing with the balance between us.

Afterwards we had a big cookout at the church fellowship room, and the whole mountain was invited. Daddy owned the only funeral home in the Gap, and everyone from there came too. I had the most fun ever, holding hands with Mark. He would take his middle finger and rub the inside of my palm, which drove me crazy. Lonnie even hung around for a while before he jumped in his brand new 1967 Ford Mustang. It was candy-apple red, and I both hated and loved him at the same time for having received such a treasure.

Not long after he left with all his buddies in tow, I overheard a conversation between Daddy and Mr. Barker, who owned the grocery in the Gap. Mark was across the yard throwing the football to my younger brothers when the word "war" filtered through my concentration.

Mr. Barker frowned, rubbing his double chin. "So he's not going to college?"

"No, some kids just don't take to school. The only thing that got Lonnie that cap and gown was him keeping his grades good so he could play football. He caught a lot of breaks. The coach even offered to help him get into Western North Carolina. Lonnie wouldn't have it."

"Do you think that is wise.? I mean with the draft?"

Daddy lit a cigarette. "I can't make him. He wants to marry Laura and work in the family business."

"He may get drafted. So many are these days."

Drafted. The very word put fear in my heart. A dark cloud hung in the distance. Paul Kincade, who lived two farms over, went to Vietnam. When he came back, he wore his hair long down his back. He never sat on a chair but instead squatted or sat on the ground. His temper had turned mean, and his mama quit the church due to folks talking about his outbursts. He sure didn't look like a solider. Daddy gave him a job when nobody else would even consider him. Mama warned Daddy to watch him close.

"Why?" Daddy had asked Mama. "Do you think he's going to kill one of our customers?" He laughed at his own joke.

Paul gave me the willies, even though I'd seen how much he thought of Daddy and Lonnie. To think Lonnie could turn out like Paul made me want my big brother to enroll in college so he couldn't be drafted.

❧

Lonnie began working for Daddy a week or two after graduation. He wore a suit and tie, with every hair in place. He turned out to be quite good at handling the grief-stricken families and the decisions they had to make. Paul ate lunch with Daddy and Lonnie every day. Daddy told Mama that Paul was becoming more social, at ease. But still he refused to cut his hair and would only wear t-shirts and jeans. I haunted the public pool down in the Gap where Mark was a lifeguard. All the girls drooled all over him, but his sight was set on me. We never did anything but kiss. Sometimes I wished we would do more. That wasn't very church-like.

On Labor Day weekend, Lonnie announced his engagement to Laura, and my parents threw a big bash at the new Chinese restaurant. Mark came with me and kept giving me knowing smiles, as if to say that one day we would be engaged too. The happy couple would marry in the spring on Laura's birthday.

Then a letter came in a real official envelope. I was the one who pulled it from the mailbox and threw it on the kitchen table with the rest of the bills and some insignificant piece of junk mail. I rushed off to cheerleading practice with only thoughts of Mark. It had become my habit to fill pages of a journal with his name in varying ways. Mr. and Mrs. Young and Mrs. Mark Young were my two favorites. So I spent that afternoon thinking of myself.

I opened the back door late that evening to find Mama holding the letter, Daddy standing over her with a stern look on his face. At first, I thought I was in trouble. I thought they had found my notebook with all the signatures and my thoughts.

"You can't open his mail," Daddy said. "He's a grown man."

Mama held the letter tight. I recognized it as the one I'd noticed earlier. "He's only eighteen."

"Any young man who receives a letter like this is a man, Martha." Daddy rarely raised his voice, but in this case it held the strain they were both feeling.

Mama didn't seem to hear him. "I have to know, Frank."

Daddy took the letter with a gentle tug. "It's not our place. We'll wait."

"Wait for what?" I took the milk from the refrigerator.

"It's too close to supper, Mary." Mama said the words without any conviction.

"So what's up with the letter?" The good thing about my family was that interruptions were bound to erupt. Right then, my twin nine-year-old brothers burst through the kitchen with muddy feet and long, flexible tree branches from outdoors. I braced myself for the onslaught of chaos this would cause, but our parents remained quiet. My brothers headed in the direction of Grandmother Owen's apartment. And that's when my world stopped turning for a minute.

"Did someone die?" I tried to sound casual.

This earned a glare from Daddy. "That was uncalled for. Help your mother with dinner." It was a death sentence for me. I hated to cook.

"Golly."

"Don't be smart." Daddy sounded madder than I'd ever hear him.

"Don't take this out on her, Frank." Mama took the letter from Daddy and leaned it against the crystal bowl on the round wooden table.

And we began preparing the longest meal of my life. I don't recall what food we cooked. I'm sure it was one of the regulars like meatloaf or fried chicken. I had no idea what was going on, or maybe I didn't want to know.

Daddy left the kitchen, but I felt him hovering somewhere just outside the door, waiting for the back door to open, waiting for Lonnie to come home. And when my big brother finally walked in the door, I wanted to give him some kind of warning, prepare him for whatever was headed his way.

Mama never turned from the stove. "Your mail is on the table."

Lonnie looked at the envelope for a long time before picking it up and tearing the seal open. He removed a single sheet of paper and read it. The world didn't fall apart, so I thought for a moment everything was fine. I watched for Lonnie to look up and laugh, squashing Mama's concerns. But his face paled and his lips became a fine thin line. Daddy picked that moment to walk into the kitchen through one of the swinging doors.

"When?" One word became a complete question.

"I report next week, Tuesday." Lonnie met Daddy's stare. Daddy's stern expression melted away, crumpled, and turned into a chiseled thought.

"Where?"

This made Mama turn from her cooking.

"Raleigh."

"What about the holidays? Isn't there something we can do about the holidays?" Mama pleaded, twisting a dishtowel.

Both Daddy and Lonnie looked at her but never spoke. They left the room at the same time, two different men but the same in many ways.

A flame leapt from the frying pan. I grabbed the dishtowel from Mama's hands and slapped at the flames as the cloth caught fire. Mama took a box of baking powder and dumped it on the flames, smothering them. One minute the fire threatened to spread, and the next it was only a hazy smoke clinging to the ceiling. The dishtowel smoldered, orange. I threw it in the sink and fought an overwhelming urge to break every plate in the kitchen.

"What's burning?" Grandmother Owen asked.

"The world is on fire," I yelled as I swung the doors open and left them to flap back and forth, back and forth. On the way up the stairs, I ran headlong into my younger sister, Teresa.

Her expression changed from her normal haughty to concerned. "What's wrong?"

"Ask Mama." I pushed past her and moved up the stairs. Lonnie was going to war. He was going to some jungle to fight. I'd seen enough on TV to know what he was walking into. Boys no older than my brother with expressions that attempted to cover their fear but couldn't quite master it. I thought of how Paul had survived and how Lonnie was much smarter. He might just make it. He had to. Pure survival pushed me out the front door, and I walked the distance to Paul's mom's farm.

I knocked. No one came. I knocked again. When no one answered, I turned to walk away. Then the door opened and Paul's mother stood there.

"I'm sorry. I was cooking. Can I help you?"

"I'm Mary. Paul works for my dad at the funeral home."

"Oh goodness, yes. I should have recognized you. Your father is such a blessing for Paul. For both of us."

"I wanted to talk to Paul."

She looked at me odd. "He's out back in the barn working on that old car of his."

Paul's hair was a tangled mess. He looked up after a couple of minutes, as if he'd been expecting me. "Hey." He looked young, not much older than me.

"What will happen to Lonnie in Vietnam? Please tell me the truth. I have to know."

He put down a wrench. "What are you talking about?"

"Lonnie got his letter today." I tried to make my voice sound angry, tough.

"I can't talk about that stuff." He turned away from me.

I grabbed his wrist and he jerked it free. "Please. I can't lose my brother. It changed you. Tell me what will happen to him."

Several different emotions crossed his face, but he settled on sternness. "I'm hungry. You can come in and eat dinner with us. I don't have a lot that will help you." He began to walk toward the house.

"Just tell me. Please."

He stopped and looked at me hard. "It's tough. I wish I could say something to make you feel better, but I can't."

"Should he run to Canada?"

"Good thought, Mary, but your brother won't do it. I wouldn't and didn't do it back when I got my letter. God, I wish now I had." He gave me a sad look. "I got a Purple Heart, but I came home another man."

"I don't want that to happen to Lonnie."

"We don't get to pick who is saved. I saw my best buddy blown to pieces. I wanted it to be me. I grabbed the soldier beside me and ran like God himself was chasing me. I got a bullet in the thigh, tore my leg up. I wanted to save everyone. I thought it was my duty." He looked at the house where a curtain moved. "Mom is collateral damage. She worries about me all the time. The only hope Lonnie has is to get stationed in Korea. Some do." Paul placed his hand on my shoulder. "I wish I'd had someone who cared half as much as you."

"Your mom cares."

"She cares, but honestly, she can't accept who I am now."

"I got to go."

He looked at me. "I'm here."

※

The day Daddy was to drive Lonnie to Raleigh, we had our first cold spell. The air reminded me of the upcoming holidays. How would we have Thanksgiving without him there? How would we sit and wait for days, weeks, months? How would we survive? How would Lonnie survive? The house that morning was quieter than the funeral home in what Daddy called a dry spell. Daddy sat in front of the TV, watching some morning show as if Lonnie had already left. We all stayed quiet, pretended it might cause more grief by acknowledging the truth.

Laura was the only honest person that week. She cried all the time. Lonnie spent a lot of his last hours at home hugging Laura, reassuring her.

On that last morning, Mama refused to leave her room. My younger brothers and sister got ready for school like any

normal day. Grandmother Owen came up the stairs to at-
tempt to speak with Mama. She spent thirty minutes
minutes talking in whispers to the closed bedroom door. Finally Mama allowed Lonnie into the room. I stood in the
hall for what seemed like an hour before he opened the door
and stepped back into the hall. My hair was ratty, and I
hadn't bathed in days. My knees went weak, but I willed myself to stand in front of him.

He held out his hand. "I'm not dead yet." And in front
of me he transformed into the old Lonnie. I laughed at his
honest statement, thinking how horrible I was to laugh.

"Geez, thanks." His face broke into a big goofy smile.
"Everyone is treating me like I'm dying from a brain tumor.
I'm just reporting for duty. Hey, we don't even know if I'll
get to go. They may find a brain tumor. We can only pray."

"I hate all this. It messes everything up."

"Sis, you're going to love driving my Mustang while I'm
gone. No more sharing a room with Teresa." He dangled the
keys in front of me. "The car has to be cranked every day.
Look after it for me." When he spoke again, it was with a
hoarse whisper. "Look after Ma and Laura. They're not
strong like you. You're made of tough stuff like me. I pity
the man you marry."

"I'm not getting married." And in that moment I realized I'd never loved Mark, and I wasn't the same person.

"You'll marry, sis. But you're going to do big things
first."

"We'll see."

He gave me a long look. "Do something big with your
life, sis."

"You're talking like you have already died."

"No way. I'm getting my Mustang back." He laughed.

228

I left the house. I couldn't watch the car pull out of the driveway.

❦

Paul opened the back door and looked me over.

"He's leaving."

He reached out and took my hand, pulling me into his mother's kitchen. "I had a long talk with Lonnie last night. He's going to be okay." Paul's voice reminded me of a sad tune playing on the radio.

"I hope so."

Paul watched me. The color of his eyes made me think of the rich brown of pecan shells. When he touched my cheek, I understood what I needed. His kisses heated my skin, and for a spilt second I thought of my silly love for Mark before the vision disappeared in our fumbling. He took me to his room. His mom had left for work already. The bridge between fantasy and reality dissolved that morning. I rode the wave of truth, or one truth, one of my truths. When Paul and I mingled into one, a sob escaped into the air around us. My former life washed away, bringing me only a pause.

I left Paul sleeping on his small bed. The air was warmer, promising to hold back winter for a while longer. I walked the mountain that day, wind blowing my hair in my face. Lonnie would never come home, and things would never be the same.

❦

A year later I was accepted into the prestigious Bellevue

229

Hospital for Nursing. I left Black Mountain after telling Mark I couldn't marry him. Lonnie never saw me become a psychiatric nurse. He never knew I married a doctor and we had three children. He never got to marry Laura, though I think he'd be pleased that she did marry and had two children.

I knew when Lonnie left the world. He came to me in a dream, wearing his army fatigues and combat boots. His smile was relaxed. "You can do anything, Mary. Remember that."

Brothers never know how much their sisters love them, the special bond they carry inside for their whole lives. I couldn't save Lonnie's life, but he saved mine. Told me the person I would become. And he was right.

LAST YEAR'S EASTER EGG

1996

Granny Alice stood up to any obstacle. When her eye wandered from her husband to the sharecropper who rented some of their land, she turned her back on common decency and encouraged his indecent attentions behind the backs of her husband, six children, and in-laws. When she decided she preferred the farmer but still wanted the money from her husband's inheritance, she used her granny witch knowledge to find a solution. Grandpa soon suffered declining health that the traveling doctor couldn't figure out. Grandpa died a painful death. The day after they planted him on the side of the mountain, Granny Alice sent all six children to the orphanage. The farmer moved into the family home that night.—Karen Lynn Nolan

Gran—propped in a hospital bed, her tissue-paper skin and droopy eyes masking the real grandmother—spoke her request with all the pride and decorum of a queen. "Could you have me for a couple of weeks? The silly doctor insists I can't stay alone. He won't release me until you agree."

"Of course you can, Gran." A warning voice went off in Alice's head. Anthony wouldn't like her rash decision.

"There is this man who keeps coming to my house, asking me questions, telling me he knows my sons." Gran's watery blue eyes gave the illusion that she was crying.

Alice knew better. "What man? What is his name?"

"I'm not sure. He just claims he knows my sons. And that big old house is so empty without Rosie." This was

Gran's lifelong friend, who had died around Christmas the year before. Gran had been headed downhill since, especially in her mind.

"I'll be back on Friday to get you. Do you want me to get anything from the farm?" Alice patted Gran's arm.

"Maybe my Bible and the picture of your grandfather."

"Any clothes, or do you have enough with you here?" Alice looked around for a suitcase-and saw none. She made a mental note to get a few housedresses and other essentials. "I'll see you Friday morning."

Gran squeezed Alice's arm with her claw-like fingers. "That husband of yours isn't going to throw a fit about me being there, is he?"

"No, Gran. Anthony loves you."

"Love don't have a thing to do with it, Alice. Men don't like sliding into second." She shook her head as if Alice was a dummy. And Alice felt second best on her good days.

⋘

"I can't do anything to help. You know how busy I am these days. The boys have to get to school and their after-school activities."

"Thank you for reminding me of my duties." Alice left her husband standing in the kitchen pouring coffee and escaped to her studio. Well, it wasn't really a studio. The room was a spare bedroom that was once a guest room, but she had claimed it as her own after she made her trip to Black Mountain that Christmas. The oil painting of the old woman hung over a small desk covered with different art supplies. The rest of the room was empty of furniture. Only a large easel stood near the French doors, which opened onto a private stone terrace that she had paid one of the locals to build. This was her place away from a life that was too much on most days. On one wall of the room was a large sheet of white paper. She had sketched raised beds and a picket fence around what would be a vegetable plot. To the right, she had drawn grapevines that ran down the long slope like an old-fashioned clothesline. To the left would be a large herb garden and flowerbeds. She picked up her phone and called her mother.

"Hello."

"Mother, I might need some help." Alice held her breath.

"What's wrong?"

"I'm going after Gran on Friday. She'll be staying here for a couple of weeks. The doctor won't allow her to leave on her own."

"Alice, you can't do this. I've worked so hard to get her into that assisted living home. She can't go back to the mountain to that rambling house." In a softer tone, she said, "Her mind is slipping. You can't allow her to talk you into things. This may hurt her more than help her."

"I just need some help with Gran while I run the boys everywhere."

"Anthony can't like the idea of your grandmother coming to stay." Mother was Gran's only child, and sometimes she sounded like the spoiled child she must have been.

"He's not the only person that lives here." Alice tapped her charcoal pencil on the desk. "This is my grandmother."

"First, Anthony may not be the only one living there, but he's the breadwinner, my dear, so be careful. Second, since when have you become so close with your grandmother?"

"She's so fragile." Alice kept her voice steady.

"Oh, she manipulated you. She's good at that."

"She keeps talking about a man who's come to the house and told her he knows her sons."

"Sons. Lord, she's going around the bend. Your grandmother can't stay alone. She's seeing and talking to people who aren't there. Don't you understand? Please don't do this."

"I said I would. She'll only be here two weeks. You can get her into the home in that length of time."

"But there is the farm. We'll have to sell it to help her stay in assisted living. This place is special. They specialize in people who have senility problems."

"She won't stand for the farm to be sold. Grandpa loved it."

"I don't know what family the farm originated with, Mom's or Dad's. Maybe they bought it together. We will be lucky to get much of anything on Black Mountain. Maybe we could find a couple looking for a getaway house." Mother was in real estate, and she was very good. "Well, if your grandmother offers you money, take it. You deserve some compensation for your trouble."

"Mother, are you listening to yourself? Would you like me to treat you that way?"

Mother took a sharp breath. "Alice, if I get in the same shape, take me out to a pasture and shoot me, put me out of my misery."

"It's not a joke. I'll never do that to you."

"Never say never. I wish I could help you, but she isn't going to stand for me to watch her while you run the boys around."

"It's fine. I'll figure it out."

"It's not too late to turn her down. Shoot, she probably doesn't even remember asking you."

Alice turned to the painting-in-progress on the easel. The woman's nose wasn't right. With a few brushstrokes, the nose transformed the woman's face into Gran's. The sound of footsteps in the kitchen reminded her to cook supper. She cleaned her brush and went upstairs without washing her hands, speckled here and there with paint.

"Mom, your hands are messy." Robbie, her ten-year-old, laughed. "Like mine." He held up dirt-encrusted fingers and nails.

"Robbie, what have you been doing?"

"Digging in the dirt. I'm going to dig a deep hole."

"Why?"

He shrugged. "Just to see if I can."

Daniel, her handsome fourteen-year-old, came into the kitchen.

Alice placed a bowl of pasta salad on the counter.

Daniel dug a spoon into the noodles and took a big bite.

"Daniel, don't eat out of the serving bowl."

"Why? It saves messing up a plate." The past few months, he'd been eating everything in the house. Sometimes she thought he was a horse grazing inside of a boy.

"Leave the boy alone." Anthony came through the back door. His voice suggested once again that he was grumpy.

"Your great-grandmother will come to stay with us tomorrow," Alice said to the boys. "I need your patience and help."

Ted, her sixteen-year-old, stuck his head around the doorframe. "I'm okay with Gran staying. Can I sleep in the den?"

"I still think it's highly inappropriate to make our son

move out of his bedroom for two weeks when you could put her in that studio. After all, she is your grandmother."

"I hate that grandmother. She always screams at me."

"She's old, Daniel." Alice tried to soothe him.

A pressure gripped her around the chest. If she had her own place, if she had never married Anthony...but that wasn't fair, and she couldn't think that way. Her sons wouldn't exist.

"I have chosen to help my grandmother. I know this is causing some changes, but please let me do this." Mostly she looked at Anthony. "I'll be leaving as soon as you guys are at school tomorrow. I have to go to the farm and get a few things. It's only two weeks."

The two-story farmhouse sat on the side of the mountain. When Alice opened the door, a feeling of pleasure washed over her. As a child, this place made her feel free of her mother and the pressure to be perfect. Gran allowed her to do pretty much what she wanted. It shouldn't take her long to gather the things on Gran's list. Then she could get Gran and head for home in time to grab Robbie from school. Her thoughts tangled around her worries, and a moaning sound went on a few moments before it finally worked through to her, into her bones. "Who is here?"

The sound stopped. A chill crawled across her scalp. Maybe a hurt animal outside or stuck in the walls. She went to the upstairs bedroom first. The room was neat as a pin, which was Gran's habit. The closet held no suitcase. Gran never went on trips. Alice pulled several housedresses off the hangers and turned to the dresser. One of the drawers was open. She was quite sure that all the drawers were closed tight when she came in. As she pushed the drawer closed, a stack of papers held by an old rubber band that had lost its stretch caught her attention. The yellowing papers crackled when she touched them. Alice, normally very conscious of privacy, pulled the pack out and shoved it in her large bag. There might be some important paperwork her mother would need to get Gran in the home. A pair of shoes, underclothes, and a couple of nightgowns finished off the list for the bedroom. Oh, and Gran's Bible. This she found on the bedside table. A few minutes later, while she was in the kitchen, the old rotary phone rang. Alice took the medicine bottles and placed them in a plastic grocery store bag. Then she picked up the phone.

"Hello?"

"Is Mrs. Riley home?" The man's voice was young. "Is this her daughter?"

"No, granddaughter."

A slight pause with a deep breath. "I'm looking to speak with your grandmother as soon as she is available."

"Can I help you?"

"I don't think so. I believe Mrs. Riley will have to be the person I speak with."

"She is ill and in the hospital. I'm not sure if she will be back here anytime soon. Do you have a number I can have?"

"Sure, and could I have a number for her?"

This seemed fair enough. They shared the numbers, and Alice hung up.

Before she left, she searched outside the house for a wounded animal but found no evidence of one.

❦

Gran, dressed in a polyester pants suit left over from the sev-
enties, waited in a wheelchair near the window. Her gnarled
arthritic hands rested in her lap. "You're late. I thought you
weren't coming." She never looked at Alice but continued to
stare out the window at the newly blooming pear trees.

"We're finally coming out of the winter," Alice com-
mented as she looked for any of the clothes Gran brought
with her.

"Child, I'll never come out of winter."

"I have to see your doctor before we go."

"Talking to him is a waste of time."

"It'll only take a minute."

The doctor held Gran's chart in his hand. "The arthritis
is debilitating. And worse, she's in the early stages of Alzheimer's. Sometimes she's completely lucid and other times
she's somewhere else. That line is blurring more and more."

"She seems mostly there today."

The doctor looked up from the chart. "I strongly suggested to your mother that Mrs. Riley needs an assisted living situation. It will allow her to stay somewhat independent
for a while. You must understand that she will have to have
full-time care one day in the near future."

The words punched the air from Alice's lungs. "Okay."

Gran complained about the coolness of Alice's house. She
complained about the light in Ted's room. The bathroom
was too far of a walk. She hated the mattress. The boys' noise
that evening caused Gran to shiver and cover her ears. Alice
convinced her to lie down before dinner and plumped the
pillows behind her head.

Gran touched Alice's arm. "You know I didn't fool nobody when I went to the granny witch."

"What do you mean, Gran?"

An aggravated expression crossed her face. "I had to get rid of him, dear. I couldn't live with him a minute longer. He wasn't mean, you know. Just dull. So, so dull. I couldn't be there with him."

"Just rest, Gran." Alice covered her with a blanket.

"I have to tell you about all this before I die." Gran closed her eyes.

"You tell me about it after supper."

Gran began to breathe deeply.

❧

Alice cooked a dinner of fried chicken and homemade biscuits, both Anthony's favorites. The table was decked out with the lace tablecloth and the new china. In the center of the farm table, she placed her daffodil bulbs, which were just opening.

Alice helped Gran walk the length of the hall to the brown leather sofa in the family room. "Here you go. Now just sit and enjoy the afternoon sun. This is one of my favorite places."

"I just hate these kind of sofas. They're cold and slippery."

"I love to read here."

"You'd better be thinking about something other than reading." Gran pinched her lips together like someone sucking on a lemon.

Alice placed a soft pillow behind Gran's back.

"Do you still paint? You always wanted to be an artist.

One of my sons was real good at drawing and such."

"You don't have a son."

"Yes, I do. You don't know it all, dearie."

Alice nodded, not sure what to say.

"Do I smell chicken cooking?"

"Yes. I thought it would be a treat."

"It's not good to eat fried foods at your age, sweetie. It goes straight to your hips." Before Alice could answer, Gran sniffed the air. "I think something is burning."

"Oh no."

"You never were much of a cook." Gran shook her head.

The biscuits were charred. As Alice took them outside before Anthony came home, the fire alarm went off. She dropped the pan of biscuits on the patio. She took the broom and knocked the cover off the fire alarm and left it on the floor. Then she walked back outside. A huge sob took her by surprise.

"Are we eating?" Anthony stood in the door.

"Yes, give me a minute." Alice didn't look at him.

Before long, Alice had served dinner, minus the bread. Gran sat at the table and frowned. "Your boys look like two of my sons."

"You had sons?" Anthony asked.

She looked at him and smiled. "Oh yes. I had four sons and two daughters. All well-mannered children. Almost too sweet and kind. Boring, if you want to know the truth."

The boys looked at Alice, surprised.

Anthony looked at her too. "Your mother is an only child."

Alice shook her head, trying to say not now. The rest of the dinner went downhill from there. Gran regaled the boys with stories about these made-up kids. "I'm just so sorry I don't know where they are now. I'd like to see them. They wouldn't want to see me."

Alice stood. "Gran, let me help you to the living area. I have some things to clean."

Gran nodded and allowed Alice to help her.

After Gran was seated, Alice went out on the patio to clean up the burnt pan and bread. The sunset was orange streaked and took away her breath. Maybe she could make it the two weeks, but Gran was harder to help than she thought.

"Do you have your grandmother out here?" Anthony stood in the kitchen door.

"Does it look like she's out here, Anthony?" Her nerves were frayed like a worn-out dish towel.

"Well, she's not in the living room. I looked everywhere but downstairs. She must have left while I went to change."

"She got out of the house?" Fear spun her thoughts.

"She's not my grandmother. I can't keep up with her."

Alice ran at Anthony. She beat his chest with fists. "She can barely walk. She has Alzheimer's."

"God, Alice, she doesn't need to be here. We can't deal with this."

"I'm your wife. This is my grandmother."

"Don't ask me to make that kind of sacrifice. I'm sorry." Anthony pushed her away. The words rode the air like a lightning bolt.

"I have to find her. Maybe you can call 911 if it's not too much trouble." She left him there and walked to the edge of the deep woods. "Gran, Gran."

"She couldn't make it all the way to the woods," Anthony yelled.

"You'd be surprised what a person can do when they put

their mind to accomplishing it." Alice walked into the woods.

Gran sat under a tree, humming, her housedress hiked up around her waist. "Look here what I found." She pushed away the leaves and pointed to the deep purple crocuses. "It's spring. He always said it was spring when you saw the cro- cuses. I killed him. I killed him without even thinking hard." She looked up at Alice. "Do I know you, young lady?"

Alice swallowed her fear. "I'm Alice. Who did you kill?"

"I was young. I couldn't stand him. He was an old man and thought about two things: working and making babies. We had six kids. I killed him and gave the six kids to the orphanage. Ain't proud of it. I married our tenant farmer. We had a girl. Now this man keeps coming around, telling me he knows my sons."

Alice remembered the man who had called.

"No one ever asked a question about that old man. They knew I threw a spell on him, killed him dead." She looked at Alice again. "You know I have a granddaughter with the name Alice, such a needy little thing. If she's not careful, she'll grow up to be a doormat to some man. I couldn't be a doormat to that old man no more."

Alice touched Gran's shoulder. "Let me help you."

"Thank you, dear. I need some help. I'm as lost as last year's Easter egg. You know, there is always one the children don't find. That's me. Last year's Easter egg."

"Me too, Gran, me too." She wouldn't tell Gran's secret. Even if the man called, she wouldn't say a word. Why would she? It wouldn't help anyone. Alice would take money from savings and buy the house on Black Mountain and move there. No one could stop her. If the boys wanted to come, they could, but she was going before something bad happened between her and Anthony.

They walked, the old woman slumped against the younger woman, back to the house, back to the choices Alice would make.

Black Mountain would save her life.